MISSIN

ALISON MOORE's first novel, *The Lighthouse*, was shortlisted for the Man Booker Prize and the National Book Awards (New Writer of the Year), winning the McKitterick Prize. Both *The Lighthouse* and her second novel, *He Wants*, were *Observer* Books of the Year. Her short fiction has been included in *Best British Short Stories* and *Best British Horror* anthologies, broadcast on BBC Radio 4 Extra and collected in *The Pre-War House and Other Stories*. Born in Manchester in 1971, she lives near Nottingham with her husband Dan and son Arthur.

*Also by Alison Moore*

NOVELS
*The Lighthouse* (2012)
*He Wants* (2014)
*Death and the Seaside* (2016)

SHORT STORIES
*The Pre-War House and Other Stories* (2013)

CHILDREN'S FICTION
*Sunny and the Ghosts* (2018)

# MISSING

ALISON MOORE

CROMER

PUBLISHED BY SALT PUBLISHING 2018

2 4 6 8 10 9 7 5 3 1

First published in Great Britain in 2018 by
Salt Publishing Ltd
12 Norwich Road, Cromer, Norfolk NR27 0AX United Kingdom

www.saltpublishing.com

Salt Publishing Limited Reg. No. 5293401

A CIP catalogue record for this book is available from the British Library

ISBN 978 1 78463 140 6 (Paperback edition)
ISBN 978 1 78463 141 3 (Electronic edition)

Typeset in Neacademia by Salt Publishing

Printed and bound in Great Britain by Clays Ltd, St Ives plc

Beneath it is all dark, it is all spreading, it is unfathomably deep; but now and again we rise to the surface and that is what you see us by.

VIRGINIA WOOLF, *To the Lighthouse*

# CONFERENCE

JESSIE CUT HER old wedding dress down to size, hemmed it just below the knee, and dyed it blue. It made a serviceable frock.

She wore it to the translation and interpretation conference in London, where they gave her a lanyard to hang around her neck, with an oversized tag that displayed her name in black capital letters. She put it on and walked slowly through the foyer of the hotel, feeling like an Elizabethan woman wearing a sign that shamed her for her wrongdoing.

After a session on machine translation, she attended the buffet lunch and attempted to mingle. It made one sound gaseous, she thought, *mingling* with the other delegates. It made one sound like breath, which brought to mind the fact, as she understood it, that with each inhalation she was drawing in atoms exhaled by the long dead.

In conversation with other delegates, she had, when listening, to keep her good ear, her right ear, turned towards whoever was talking. In her left ear, she had lost all hearing. This happened, sometimes, after swimming: the water caused her to go deaf on one side or the other. Usually, after a few hours or a day, something gave or popped and everything went back to normal. Occasionally, though, this did not happen; the pressure was different and she knew that there would be no give, no pop, no going back to normal. She would have to make an appointment with the surgery, see a nurse, and then she would have to do that awkward thing with oil: her husband used to do it for her, drizzling the warmed oil into her earhole while she lay on her side, very still, anticipating the relief. Now she would have to do it herself, and most likely she would misjudge it and flood the earhole; the cooling oil would ooze down her jaw, circle her neck, stain her pillowcase.

Being deaf in even one ear made her feel disconnected, distant, not quite part of the real world. Speaking, she found herself stumbling over her words, which had become, inside her head, muffled, hazy at the edges; they seemed trickier to use. She tried to put them right but could not really see that it mattered; she began to prefer to say nothing at all. She had been this way since the end of October, since before the Halloween party that she had attended with Isla and Andy from next door. Jessie had gone as someone who had died of tuberculosis. She had fake blood trickling from her mouth, and fake blood on a handkerchief that she carried. A child had asked her what she had come as, and Jessie replied, 'I died of tuberculosis.' But it was noisy – there was a DJ playing 'Devil Woman' – and when the child came back and when other children came and spoke to her, asking questions from down there, their heads at the height of her hips, her belly, she could not really hear them, so she simply said again, 'I died of tuberculosis.' After a while, the children stopped coming over, stopped asking her questions.

Now, too, in the conference hall with her plate of buffet food, Jessie was unable to follow the conversation, even with her good ear: all she could hear was the sound of her own eating filling her head.

In the afternoon, there were more sessions, with a break for coffee, and in the evening there were pre-dinner drinks and the dinner, and finally Jessie was able to withdraw upstairs to her hotel room and close the door.

She looked for a face. It had become a habit, having to find the faces in strange rooms; she had to do it or she would not be able to settle, she would not be able to sleep. She found one in the en suite bathroom, on the back of the door, in a knot in the wood: a long face – it looked as if it were melting, howling.

The house in Hawick, which had been her home for thirteen years, had very likely revealed all of its faces now. There were dozens of them; they seemed to come out of the woodwork, or she found them in the pattern of the linoleum on the bathroom floor. One was cast on a wall when the sun shone through a certain window at a certain angle; another appeared after dark, when Jessie turned on a particular lamp which threw shadows on the wall above the mantelpiece.

The cat and the dog would be missing her, although the cat would be keeping itself busy. It was a killer, that cat; it was a demon mouser. The dog would just be waiting. Isla and Andy's seventeen-year-old son Alasdair was coming round from next door twice a day to feed them and to walk the dog. Jessie had not been away overnight since the start of the year, and this conference had almost been upon her before she realised that she was going to have to ask someone to see to the animals. Her first thought had been Alasdair. She had gone next door and knocked and it was Alasdair who answered. 'Mum's not in,' he said.

'That's OK,' said Jessie. 'It's you I want. Can I come in?' Alasdair looked uncertain but he let her inside and she followed him into the living room. He sat down and resumed a computer game that he had been playing. Jessie sat down next to him and watched him for a while: he went through a portal, to somewhere quite different, to another kind of world. She asked him, 'Do you play this a lot?' Some of them played these computer games for hours every day; it was a long time to spend in an imagined world, beyond the screen. He did not hear her: he was absorbed; he was miles away. She tried again; she said his name: 'If you go through a portal, Alasdair, can you come back through?'

Without taking his eyes from the screen, he said, 'Well, you can,' and he tried to explain but she did not really understand how it worked. Sometimes, it seemed, you could not get back through, or at least you could not come back the same way you went in.

Jessie used to like stories in which you could go through a doorway into some secret and lovely place: *The Secret Garden*, in which, in a wakening garden, a boy believed to be crippled was brought back to health; and *The Pied Piper of Hamelin*, in which,

> *as they reached the mountain-side,*
> *A wondrous portal opened wide,*

and the children were let into a beautiful land,

> *Where waters gushed and fruit-trees grew,*
> *And flowers put forth a fairer hue,*
> *And everything was strange and new.*

In that story too there was a boy who was lame, and who hoped, on the far side, in the beautiful land, to be cured, only he could not get in.

When she was older, she read these same stories to Eleanor,

whom Jessie had always called her favourite niece even though she was her only niece, her only sibling's only child. Even that was going back more than thirty years now. She wondered whether they were still read, these medieval and pre-war stories. Abridged versions of children's classics seemed to be popular now.

Jessie recalled a nightclub that she used to go to when she was a student. It was inside what looked, from the outside, like an ordinary house. It had no signage but had an old-fashioned lamp shining above the door. She had gone back recently, and found that she could no longer tell which door was the right one: there were many with lamps above them; she had never noticed that before. She would no longer have known which door to knock on; she would no longer have been able to get into the club, except perhaps by walking the length of the street knocking on all those doors. Besides, that was going back thirty years as well; the club was probably no longer there.

'I wanted to ask you, Alasdair,' she said, 'if you would look after the animals for me, just for a few days: feed them, and walk the dog. I have to go to a conference in London.' She wasn't sure if he'd heard her; he stared at the screen, intent on his fantasy world. 'I'll pay you,' she added. She watched his thumbs moving fast around the remote control; she had no idea what he was doing. She was about to ask again, to say, 'Alasdair?' when he said, 'All right.'

She gave him a spare key to her house, and her mobile number, and she put his number into her phone.

She had been texting him from the hotel in London, asking him how the animals were. Worrying that the dog might think she had abandoned it, she had asked Alasdair to set up a Skype session between her and the dog, so that it could hear her voice, but when, arriving at the hotel, she had tried it, she had found that it just upset the dog because it could hear her but it could not find her.

Alasdair never saw the cat, he said, but he knew it was there because the food he put down always went; and once, when he had been out all day himself and came in late to do the supper and the dog walk, he heard something, a scratching noise, coming from one of the upstairs rooms. When he went to look, he did not see the cat, but it was not the dog, which did not leave his side.

Jessie had heard the scratching too; she had heard it even when the cat – soft and silent and dark like the night – was fast asleep on the bed.

When Jessie was a little girl, in Cambridgeshire, she had once gone for a bath and found a mouse scurrying about at the tap end. She knew very well that it was a mouse but in the playground she said that it was a rat, perhaps just for the drama of it, or perhaps because that better described how it felt, the sight of that hairy thing scuttling around the rim of the bright white bath, looking for a gap to squeeze through, while Jessie stood there in the nip.

Perhaps the scratching was the sound of a mouse that the cat had yet to kill, or perhaps it was a bird, or birds. They could get in between the walls.

In the hotel bathroom, she ran herself a deep, hot bath, hoping it would help her to sleep. She placed her open laptop in the doorway so that she could listen to music, an ambient playlist, although once she was in the bath she found that she could hardly hear it. She trimmed her softened toenails and scrubbed her softened skin. When the water cooled, she ran the hot tap again and then lay soaking, trying not to splash, straining to hear a muffled 'Keep On Loving You', the Cigarettes After Sex cover of the REO Speedwagon track that she remembered from her teens.

Before getting into bed, she got down on her knees, clasped her hands together and said, 'Forgive me.' She had done this for years, for decades, and she would not stop now, even if no one was listening.

She was plagued by sleepless nights. She read in bed until she could hardly keep her eyes open and then, night after night, she lay in the dark, waiting for sleep to come, while the hours slowly passed. She had dark circles under her eyes.

Her current reading was a biography of D. H. Lawrence. She had read two others before this one; this was her third life of Lawrence. In what she had read of his work, there was always a sense of being poised between worlds, between what Lawrence referred to as 'the old England and the new', between the old rural way of life and the new industrial way of life, or between being stuck working in a factory and making some kind of artistic breakthrough. The characters that Jessie supposed to be him, really, in fictional form, were always torn between staying and leaving, torn between this world, this life, and another.

Jessie was reading the Lawrence biography a chapter at a time, trying to eke it out. It would not be very long before Lawrence had to die all over again. His body would grow terribly thin, and he would not know where he was, where his hands were, and Frieda would sit by the bed, holding the ankle of his wasted leg, holding his bones, while he died. The sadness that this caused in Jessie was like a weight on her lungs, like when the cat curled up on her chest in the night.

For now, though, Lawrence was still alive, still young and full of vigour, a boy living at home and in love with his mother. Jessie inserted the bookmark, placed the book on the bedside table and tried to sleep.

Before breakfast, Jessie took a hot shower and then dealt with her hair. She straightened it religiously, smoothing it until it looked – held taut between her scalp and the tongs – like a sheet of brushed copper, as if she were a statue in the process of becoming copper coated. It would still kink, though, as the day wore on; the stubborn family curls would push through, like the strands of grey she kept finding.

Putting the straighteners down on the dressing-table-cum-desk, she happened to glance at the notepad that was put out for guests to use. She could see the imprint of a previous guest's handwriting: I AM HERE, it said. Next to the notepad was the hotel information pack, with cursive print on the cover saying, HOW CAN WE HELP? She left the straighteners to cool and went down to breakfast.

The day's programme began at nine o'clock. After a morning session on overcoming barriers in translation, Jessie went into the lunchroom, where she alternated between struggling to get a grip on the conversation and simply saying, 'I'm sorry but I really can't hear you.' She felt once again like a ghost saying to small children, 'I died of tuberculosis.' The programme finished before teatime, but Jessie sloped off early, skipping the afternoon sessions, as well as another evening of socialising and another night in a strange room, and instead heading for the train station.

She remembered being young and missing the last train home, and having to wait around on the platform for hours and hours until the first train of the next morning. She would have been eighteen; she would have been in between school and university. Eighteen seemed so young to her now; at that age, she had been so irresponsible. But at the same age, her mother had been married, with a brand-new baby.

Jessie once asked her mother, 'Does having babies hurt?'

Her mother laughed and said, 'Of course it hurts.' But, she said, she had got through it by imagining that by pushing out the baby, she was pushing out the pain. 'That's just the start of it though,' she said. 'You'll find out for yourself one day.'

At Euston, she headed for a concession to see if there was anything she fancied. As Jessie was about to go inside, a woman standing at the entrance reached out and grasped Jessie's wrist with long, thin fingers. In her other hand, the woman was holding out a takeaway cup of tea, offering it. The woman did not look at all well. Jessie had once accepted a paper cup of cider that had been passed her way by strangers at a party. She had taken a sip and at that same moment thought, *There could be anything in this*. It was a basic rule – *Don't accept sweets from strangers* – but as she swallowed the questionable cider she realised that she had essentially done just that. She had been fine – it really was just cider, probably, although she had drunk no more of it, and had instead abandoned the cup on a windowsill.

'No, thank you,' said Jessie, although she smiled at this woman, in whose grip the unwanted cup of tea was vibrating slightly, and on whose back sat a huge and terribly heavy-looking orange rucksack. Jessie turned away and went inside. She bought herself a cup of tea, a tuna sandwich and a magazine, and then headed for her platform and the train which would take her to Carlisle. In Carlisle, she would have a wait of just under an hour before the bus came. She would get herself a warm drink and maybe stretch her legs, and then she would catch the bus; it would take her all the way to Hawick, and in Hawick she would walk to her house and shut her front door.

She found her train, her carriage, her seat; she was pleased to have a window seat, even though much of the journey would be spent in darkness, into which she would be travelling as if into a tunnel; it would be rather like spending endless hours on the underground.

She enjoyed train travel. The previous summer – not this year, whose summer seemed barely to start before ending, but the one before – she had taken a series of trains down through England, into France, and then northeast into Germany. Years earlier, she had taken an interest in the work of a German author of children's picture books, though her own childhood was long gone: she was in her thirties then, working as a freelance translator, and her first marriage was coming to an end. In one of the picture-book stories, a mother causes her child to fly apart. The pieces are flung into the sky and the sea, into the mountains and the city; they have to be found again, and sewn back together. *Entschuldigung*, says the mother, at the end: *Excuse me* or, in this context, *I'm sorry*. Another story is about a dying man who since childhood has had an angel looking over his shoulder, and nothing ever hurts him. Jessie loved these books, and would have liked a child to share them with now, but she did not have one. The author lived in Hamburg, and when Jessie had come across what seemed to be the author's postal address, she had sent her a letter, written in German. The address must have been old, though, or somehow wrong, because the letter was returned, with a sticky label (*Empfänger nicht zu ermitteln*) informing her that the addressee could not be traced. Jessie had found that authors in general could be very hard to get in touch with, hidden as they often were behind the veil of an agent or a publisher.

By the time she took that train trip to Germany, she was in her late forties, and travelling with her second husband, Will. He had been a train driver, a train enthusiast, and she had hoped that the expedition would do him good, but he had spent the hours silently straining to see the track, to see what lay ahead, around the bends; it had perhaps been a mistake.

They visited Hamburg, where Jessie thought again about this author, and wondered whether she still lived in the city; if so, Jessie might have been within a few miles of her. It might as well have been a few thousand miles though, seeing as Jessie still did not know the author's address. Then one afternoon, walking down by the river with Will, Jessie thought she glimpsed her, or someone very much like her, or very much like the pictures she had seen of her, and she followed her for some time, for some way, hurrying on ahead of Will, trying to catch up. The woman was quite a walker, pressing on when Jessie paused with a stitch in her side, and eventually Jessie lost her, or perhaps it had never been her at all. Looking around, Jessie realised that she had come a long way from Hamburg's centre, that she was far from the area marked on her tourist map. She began the walk back.

She opened her magazine and flipped through it, glancing at headlines and pictures. She looked at a page of winter coats:

trench coats and duffle coats in the shades of a violent sunset; they were streaks of fire-engine red, scarlet, shocking pink, blood red and fish-finger orange. She donated her old magazines to surgery waiting rooms. Some of the magazines you found in waiting rooms were years out of date. She would find herself in a waiting room one day, leafing through this same magazine, looking at these same winter coats, which would no longer be available.

An announcement was made over the tannoy, confirming where they were going, so that no one would end up somewhere they had not meant to be; and then the train was pulling out, although Jessie had not heard the whistle – wasn't there always a whistle, which let you know that the train was going to move? They had those lollipops as well, that they held up to signal to the driver, to say something like, *It's safe to go now.*

Looking up, looking out of the window, she saw that where another train had come in on an adjacent track there was some kind of commotion, something was wrong. People were gathering on the platform, and Jessie saw the orange rectangle of a huge rucksack, abandoned near the edge of the platform, just where all those people were standing, looking down onto the track.

As Jessie's train pulled out of the station, she leant into the aisle, looking up and down the carriage, but everyone else in there seemed to be busy with their newspapers and phones and children and meal deals. Jessie turned back to the window, but the orange rucksack and the group around it were no longer visible.

She wanted a guard to come into the carriage so that she could ask what had happened, but there would not be one on this train; their tickets had been checked at the barrier. She thought of the ticket inspector on a train that she used to catch regularly, who, as he walked down the aisle, checking tickets, would say to each passenger, 'Thank you,' except that he clipped his speech like he clipped the tickets so that what he actually said was, 'You.' He would advance down the carriage, coming towards Jessie, saying, 'You . . . You . . . You . . .' He would stop beside her, take her ticket and give it back with a hole punched through, and go on down the carriage, saying, 'You . . . You . . . You . . .'

The magazine was still on her lap, open at those coats that she had been looking at when whatever had happened had happened. She put the magazine aside and did not pick it up again.

There was graffiti spray-painted on the brickwork that ran alongside the train tracks – people left messages, or just their own names, so that someone would see it and know that they had been there. She tried to read them all but already the train was travelling too fast; the graffiti went by before she could fasten her eyes onto it.

They passed the old Ovaltine factory. She ought to try Ovaltine, to see if it might help her to sleep. The former factory had been turned into housing; she was not sure where Ovaltine was manufactured now, or indeed if it still was.

They passed through miles and miles of countryside, as dusk gathered over it. Each time they stopped at a station, the announcement was made, to let everyone know where the train was going, but by then they were moving again and if anyone was on the wrong train it was too late to get off.

A man sitting across the aisle from Jessie opened some foil-wrapped sandwiches. You did not see that very often these days, grown-ups eating homemade sandwiches. They looked like the sandwiches that her sister used to make for ferry crossings. She used square bread and thick slices of orange cheese, Red Leicester. The foil-wrapped squares looked like an astronaut's meal. As children, Jessie and Gail had eaten quite peculiar fillings: brown sugar sandwiches when they got home from school, lettuce and ketchup sandwiches on a nudist beach. She remembers looking up from that nudist-beach sandwich and seeing an elderly man in a three-piece suit, a watch chain hanging between the pockets of his waistcoat, polished shoes on his feet. He was standing in the middle of the beach, looking perplexed. He had presumably been walking but had come to a stop and was looking around him at all the nudists, and then up and down the length of the beach. The nudist section extended for perhaps half a mile in either direction. He looked as if he did not know how he had come to be there, as if he had just stepped through a hole in time, and Jessie pictured a parlour somewhere in which a modestly dressed lady was wondering where he had gone. Jessie remembered finding grains of sand in her sandwich.

The passenger with the homemade sandwiches had a plaster on his forefinger, which he was carefully holding away from the bread. Jessie imagined him in his kitchen, slicing a tomato, the knife going into his flesh, the sting of tomato juice in the wound, and him having to see if he had a plaster in the bathroom cabinet. The plaster he was wearing was one of the old-fashioned kind: it was the same colour as his skin, barely noticeable. Gail had kept happier plasters in her first-aid kit, with smiling Mr Men and smiling spacemen and smiling aliens on them. They did help, apparently: smiling worked as a painkiller. She tried it now, turning her head to the window to pull her mouth into a smile. The darkness outside had turned the window into a mirror, and in it she caught the eye of the man with the homemade sandwiches, who smiled back at her. Jessie shifted her gaze and for the rest of the journey she avoided looking his way.

As they travelled north, she heard the accents changing around her, and somewhere in between Kendal and Penrith it started to rain. She had a childhood memory of standing at the edge of rainfall, and running in and out of it. She remembered it like a curtain of rain, the chilly plunge like running through a waterfall, or like crashing through a thin sheet of ice into freezing cold water. Probably it had not been like that at all; probably the edge had been hazy and spitty, the difference in temperature negligible. It was somewhere in the Hope Valley, a lovely part of the world. She could not recall the precise location, though she tried, as if remembering would enable her to go back and run into the rain again, in and out.

# 1985

WHEN JESSIE PLAYED childminder to her big sister Gail's little girl, Eleanor always wanted Jessie to help her build a den. When the den was finished, Eleanor always wanted Jessie to sit inside it with her and read stories. It was dim inside these dens, and if Jessie could not see the words on the page, she missed bits out or made bits up. She expected Eleanor to notice, but she never did.

Eleanor's favourite story was a picture book about Frogmen: amphibious creatures that lived in the vast, deep sea but sometimes surfaced and came onto the land and might be glimpsed in the distance, or might come so terribly close that you could see their nostrils and smell the salt water on their skin. All these Frogmen lived alone, and they were lonely, but in the end, in the final pages of the picture book, they began to find one another, and to make friends, and to fall in love.

Jessie always felt that there was something rather disturbing about the story. On holiday with Gail and her family, on the beach as the sun went down, Jessie thought about the Frogmen and could not decide whether she would want to see the smooth head of one rising above the water, the webbed feet stepping onto the wet sand. She imagined the slapping sound that the Frogman's feet would make as it came towards her. She would not know whether to welcome it or turn and run. She watched the water and shivered.

It was the first time Gail and Gary had invited Jessie – who was eighteen that year – to join them on their family holiday; and as it turned out, it was also the last time, the only time. They had been on the ferry, midway between England and France, and had eaten their cheese sandwiches, when Eleanor asked to go up on deck, so Jessie took her. It was blustery, but they found somewhere to sit. Eleanor wanted her aunt to read her the Frogman book which was in her backpack, so they got it out. They were still near the beginning when Eleanor pulled the book towards herself, to better see a picture. Jessie let go, but Eleanor must not have been holding it properly. The book fell through the railings and into the sea.

'You let go!' cried Eleanor.

'I thought you had it,' said Jessie.

'*You* were supposed to be holding it,' said Eleanor.

They looked down at the choppy water, but already they could not see the book.

'Perhaps a Frogman will find it,' said Jessie, but she could tell that even Eleanor, who was only five, knew that was highly unlikely.

# CONNECTION

I FEEL AS *if I've been away for years. I've been existing without a watch, without a calendar; I've felt timeless, though time has passed regardless.*

*I found myself waking up feeling homesick and thinking of Jessie, and I decided I would send her a message; I would tell her: I'm on my way home.*

WHEN JESSIE EMERGED from Carlisle train station, it was not quite six o'clock but it felt like the middle of the night. On the far corner of Botchergate, there was a cafe bar. Jessie crossed the road and went inside, grateful for the warm lighting and the friendly face behind the bar. She ordered a scone and a pot of tea and took a seat at the window, facing the station and the bus stops, with the bar's music and chatter behind her. She spread her scone with butter and strawberry jam and poured her tea. She had not realised how hungry she was until she started eating. She wolfed down her scone. There was a little square of flapjack on her saucer; it was a nice touch, a kindness for which she was grateful.

Feeling replenished, she decided to take a walk before catching the bus and having to sit again. She put on her coat, picked up her shoulder bag and her travel bag and headed out into the dark evening. She walked down Botchergate. Seeing a man coming towards her, she was aware of bracing herself for some comment. Once, a man in a city centre had said to her, as he passed her, 'Bitch.' She had not known the man; she had not even seen his face. Who would say such a thing, she thought, to a stranger? She had been minding her own business. But still, 'Bitch,' he said.

The man on Botchergate passed her without comment, and Jessie went on past the shopfronts. Where the doorways were set back, she half-expected to find someone sleeping, or underage teenagers drinking things with names like Mad Dog and Wicked. But the doorways were empty; the homeless and the children were elsewhere.

Jessie walked down as far as the evangelical church, where she stopped and looked at her watch and realised that she ought in fact to be heading for the bus stop. She turned back and retraced her steps.

In between a pub and the cafe bar, a little girl was toing and froing beneath a street lamp, running into and out of the wash of orange light. With an outstretched hand, the child seemed to be trying to touch the lamplight and then – as if to see if it felt any different – the darkness. Jessie wondered what on earth the child was doing out on her own, at this time of night, in this cold weather. Jessie had drawn close enough to put a hand on the child's shoulder – her hand had already begun to move, and what would she say, *Come with me, I'll buy you something, warm you up, keep you safe?* – when a woman emerged from the darkness and took the child's hand and the child skipped away with her.

Jessie was nearly at the crossing when the door of the cafe bar opened and a man came out. He stepped into her path, stopping her in her tracks. 'Excuse me,' said Jessie, beginning to move around him without really looking at him, looking down, noticing his brogues.

'Pardon me,' said the man, and Jessie glanced up at him. He looked like a spiv adrift in time. 'I know your face,' he said, pointing a finger at her. 'I'm just trying to place you.'

'I'm sorry,' said Jessie. 'I have to go. I have to catch my bus.'

'Jessie Noon,' said the man. She might have denied it, had it not been for the conference name tag that was still hanging from her neck in its shiny, protective sleeve, visible through the unbuttoned opening of her coat and lit by the light from the bar. 'That sounds like the name of a cowboy.'

'I'm not a cowboy,' said Jessie. She looked automatically for this man's name tag, but of course he was not wearing one. 'Do I know you?'

'I'm Robert,' said the man, extending a hand. Jessie kept one hand on her travel bag and one hand around the bunch of keys in her coat pocket. 'I've seen you,' he said, 'in The Bourtree in Hawick. You're often in there.'

'It's my local,' said Jessie.

'You're not from Hawick.'

'I am,' she insisted.

'You don't have a Scottish accent.'

'I grew up in Cambridgeshire,' she said. 'I moved to Hawick thirteen years ago.'

'You've settled there then.'

'Yes,' said Jessie.

'Whereabouts?'

'Just off the High Street,' said Jessie. 'Near the Horse.' As soon as she had said this, she thought that she ought not to have done; she did not know this man, who would now know where to find her. She excused herself; 'I have a bus to catch,' she said. She moved around him – and he did make her move around him; he made no attempt to get out of her way.

On the corner, waiting to cross over to the bus stop on English Street, she glanced back, and saw that he had gone.

On the bus, she sat in front of a youth who was listening to music through headphones. Jessie could only hear the tinny edges of tracks which, as the miles went by, she failed to identify; even so, she thought that the music must have been very loud in the young man's ears, and she worried about his ear drums and the possibility of perforation.

The bus followed the A7 all the way to Hawick. When it crossed the border, Jessie recalled Eleanor's bewilderment at crossing the invisible border between France and Belgium; how inconceivable it was that they could have slipped so silently into a different country. Perhaps she would always think of Eleanor when she crossed a border.

Jessie had felt just the same way when she travelled from Cambridgeshire up to the Scottish Borders all those years ago. Hours had gone by, and still she had been travelling, on and on, further and further north, and she had kept thinking that she must be in Scotland now, but she had not seen a sign; but perhaps, she thought, she had just been looking the other way. It had felt most peculiar, not to know which country she was in; besides, there was so often a gap in between the sign that said you were now leaving one place – a town or a county or a country – and the sign that said you were now entering another place. Jessie had always wondered about these gaps, which were like stretches of lawless wilderness. And then she saw it: the SCOTLAND *welcomes you* sign, and she could have wept.

She had come to a country that the ancient Romans had struggled to conquer, for all their marching along their long, straight roads, for all their armies, for all the noise of their heavy boots.

It was the first time she had been into Scotland since childhood, when she had spent an Easter week at Loch Ness with her parents and Gail. They had taken a detour on their way home, driving down a side street in Hawick. Her dad stopped the car outside an old house and said, 'That's where your great-great-grandmother lived.' From the back seat of the car, with the window wound down, Jessie had seen a woman in an upstairs room, standing at the lowered sash window, looking out. Ever since then, this woman had been inextricably linked in Jessie's mind with the great-great-grandmother she had never met and who was long dead even as she met that woman's eye through the open windows.

Years later, Jessie had looked up her great-great-grandmother, Lenore, in the census records. She found her still alive in all the records up to 1891, after which she disappeared. She could not find a death certificate, or any further mention of her. She did not know if Lenore had made it into the twentieth century.

She had, of course, more than one great-great-grandmother: she had eight of them, a good number for a dinner party, she thought. She imagined having them all over, all the great-great-grandmothers, and cooking a huge lasagne for them. Mentally, she sat them down around her dining table – it would necessitate putting the extra leaf in the table to make it long enough, and she would have to bring in the piano stool and a couple of folding garden chairs so that there would be enough seats. Their faces were fuzzy; their colours were muted – they were monochrome and sepia. Their necklines were high and their skirts were long. She knew only snippets about them: one had been taken to see a king when she was little but did not know until afterwards that she *had* seen the king, because she had been looking for somebody wearing a crown, not an ordinary hat. Another one had gone to Cambridge to see Queen Victoria and came home saying that she had only seen the backs of other people's heads. This was mostly what Jessie knew of her great-great-grandmothers, these tales of them trying to glimpse royalty. It wasn't much, but these were the things, these little stories, that had survived into the twenty-first century.

It was early in the new century that, newly divorced and briefly Jessie Noon again, she had found the Hawick house for sale online. She had recognised it, and began at once to put into motion her move up north. When she crossed the border, it was summertime and everything was green. Now it was autumn and the leaves were orange and falling.

The walls of the house still held the gas light fixtures from Lenore's day, although they no longer worked; they had been painted over, painted the same colour as the walls, and Jessie had draped some fairy lights over them. There had been people in the house since Lenore of course, including the woman Jessie had seen at the window when she was a child. Talking to Isla, Jessie had wondered aloud whether a house might remember past occupants, whether it might miss them. Isla said, 'I wouldn't have thought so,' and went back to pegging out her washing. But Jessie liked how connected she felt to Lenore in her house, and she did feel welcome in the town.

During her first year in Hawick, Jessie had met Will, who at the time was separating from his first wife. Within months, he and his dog had moved in with Jessie; she had married him quickly, as if there were a child, though there was not. They got married in a register office without inviting anyone they knew; they had strangers for witnesses. The early anniversaries hardly sounded real: paper, fruit, salt, tin. Then, after thirteen years together, he had walked out.

Will had never liked Jessie's books; he did not like to live with so much stuff; he did not like the way that all this stuff, all her books, gathered dust. Free surfaces attracted piles of books, and bare walls attracted shelves which filled with books, which attracted dust. He did read, but he did not like books. Jessie had once got him a biography that he had been wanting; she got it out of the library and when he opened it he found a stranger's crumbs in the hinge, nestled between the pages, and was infuriated.

The routine of Jessie's days and weeks was much the same now as it had been during their marriage, as it had been before their marriage: she woke at fifteen minutes to seven, lay in bed until seven, and then got up, took a shower, made a cup of tea, ate fruit for breakfast. She was not sure whether the routine helped or not when it came to missing Will, whose presence lingered in the shape of the dog that he had not taken with him, and the shirts of his that still hung in his half of the wardrobe, and the coat of his that still hung on a peg near the door, and the things in the freezer that only he ate but which she had not thrown away, and so many other things, and yet he was not there. What was more, she did not know where he was, and might never know again.

The morning he left – when, at a quarter to seven, the clock radio shocked her back into the land of the living – Jessie lay in bed and listened to the news of the discovery of a roundhouse from the Bronze Age, from so many hundreds of years Before Christ, when the people had gods, of course, but not God, not the God she knew, or had thought she did. She had, at times, taken a passing interest in other gods. She had favourites: the Hindu Trimurti, in which destruction and creation were two faces of one being; and Janus, the Roman god of doorways and thresholds; and Odin, the Norse god of death and healing.

The roundhouse was on stilts, perfectly preserved. There had been a catastrophic event – a fire, something like that – and people had left in a hurry as they did at Pompeii; they left their food bowls where they fell. There was a single human skull. This had happened in the Cambridgeshire Fens, not far from where she used to live.

Will left in the middle of winter, and now winter was coming again. At first, people had kept asking where he was, and she sometimes thought they asked in a way that made her sound responsible, as if she had been careless with him, or as if she might be keeping him trapped somewhere in the house. But after a while, word got around; he was known to have left, and people stopped asking about him. When Will had been gone for nine months, Jessie began using her own name again. Some people, elsewhere, had only ever known her as Jessie Noon anyway, and some still knew her by her first married name. In different circles, she was known by different names.

She missed him most first thing in the morning, when she had only one cup of tea to make, and when she walked the dog, especially in the evening, when she liked to hear about his day and tell him about hers, and when she sat down to eat alone, and in bed, before sleeping. She brought her work and her books into bed instead. She was reading less fiction than she used to; she found herself wanting non-fiction, facts, real people. She had read a book about scientists recording the faint sound of two black holes colliding more than a billion years ago, the collision causing waves that could still be detected now. People were always finding things that you had not realised anyone was looking for. She would not even have known where to start.

# 1985

'BUT HOW CAN we be in a different country?' Eleanor asked, and kept asking. She needed there to be a barrier that had to be raised to let them through, or a guard to observe their crossing from one territory to the other, or at the very least a visible line to cross, but there was not even that.

'You can just drive from one country to the other,' said Gail. 'You can't see the border.'

Was there even a sign to say that they had entered Belgium? Jessie had not seen one. There was just, here and there, some slight difference – the language on the motorway signs suggested that they had crossed over.

They drove for some hours, while Eleanor nibbled on crackers to stave off travel sickness. They spent the first half of the journey playing car games: they played I Spy, though the things Eleanor chose were never big, obvious things like the sky or the road, or things that were travelling right along with them like her parents or the windscreen; she chose the most obscure things, which were already out of sight by the time Jessie started guessing. Jessie failed again and again, and said that Eleanor was not playing fairly, and then Eleanor refused to play at all.

Eleanor spent the second half of the journey seeing how long she could hold her breath, though Gail did not like her doing this and had to keep telling her to stop.

Eleanor said to Jessie, 'I can hold my breath for a hundred seconds.'

'That's a long time,' said Jessie.

'I could hold it for longer,' said Eleanor.

If you looked, you could see her doing it: she got a certain expression on her face, although Jessie was not really paying attention; she was gazing out of the window at the world going by. She heard her sister saying, 'Stop it, Eleanor,' and she heard Eleanor's breath coming out. Eleanor would gnaw on another cracker or try to see shapes in the clouds, and then she would do it again, going silent, stiffening, her eyes going blank.

# COMMUNICATION

*I*'VE BEGUN THE *long journey home. I travel through time zones, the climate changing around me, and as I make my way I'm sending messages, to let her know I am coming, to say that I will be there soon.*

I T WAS JUST after eight in the evening when the bus arrived at the Mart Street stop in Hawick, just past The Baby Shop. Some people stood up early, ready, but Jessie waited for the bus to come to a standstill, fearful of sudden braking.

It was not too late to pop into Morrisons, and Jessie did so, wanting apples and milk. She got more shopping than she had meant to, and stood in a queue at the checkout with her basket precariously overfilled. She would be able to put her basket down and unpack it when the woman in the navy coat in front of her moved forward. Jessie stood, with everything balanced. It was only when the woman in the navy coat turned very slightly to the side, so that Jessie could see the outline of her forehead, her cheekbone, her jaw, that she realised who it was. Jessie started to turn and move away, but the movement caused the shopping in her basket to shift; a tin that had seemed safe on top of a packet of raisins now rolled over the edge of her basket and onto the floor. The noise caused the woman in navy to glance in her direction before turning away again. 'Hello,' said Jessie. She knew the woman's name, which was Kirstin, but she did not feel able to use it as they had never actually been introduced. And was it Kirstin, not Kirsteen or Kristen? She was unsure. The woman in navy was busy with her shopping now; she was fetching a voucher out of her purse. Jessie had no idea if she had recognised her or if she realised that it was her to whom Jessie had been speaking. The greeting hung in the air between them. Jessie picked up her tin and returned it to her basket. She thought about moving to another checkout, but she stayed put, gripping her basket with both hands, her arms aching.

From the supermarket, it was only a short walk, a few minutes, to her door. She passed the Congregational Church, admiring it. It was a beautiful structure, a listed building. She had never gone inside. She had thought about doing so many times, but had never yet climbed the stone steps to the imposing double doors. She imagined the iron ring of the door handle, cold to the touch, turning under her hand; she imagined the weight and creak of the door as she pushed it open, and the hush on the far side.

At her front door, she took her keys out of her coat pocket and slid the door key into the lock, thinking how lovely that was, to have a key that fitted a lock, a key that turned and opened the door and let her inside. You heard about people changing their locks so that those who had left them could not return, could not come back for their belongings. She imagined Will coming home and finding the locks changed. She would not do that.

She carried her travel bag over the threshold and closed the door behind her. She had once read a true story about a woman whose house burnt down and who had no home insurance, and Jessie had thought that if that happened to her she would take enough money out of the bank to buy a campervan, an old one, whatever she could afford – leaving enough in her account for petrol and food – and she would live on the move. Now she knew that she would not do that;

now she knew she needed walls and ceilings, ones that stayed put. She would not be able to stand it, forever arriving in places that she did not know, always having to look on a map to know where she was, feeling like a runaway, every morning waking up and having to remember.

On the doormat, there was some mail addressed to the previous occupant of the house, whom Jessie had never met, and there was a postcard from Gail. Jessie was always surprised that her sister could bear to speak to her. She was glad to get these postcards, with some pleasant picture on the front and *Love from Gail* on the back. Gary's name was missing, though he would be there too. They were not far from home in fact; they were still in East Anglia, but spending a week on the coast. It was a funny time of year to choose, Jessie thought – November was rather cold for a week of English seaside – but of course they no longer had to stick to the school holidays.

Jessie had not seen Gail since New Year, after making a last-minute decision to accept the invitation to Gail and Gary's New Year's Eve party. Jessie had worn her silver trouser suit, and silver shoes, and Gail had said that she looked like a spaceman, and Jessie thought that maybe she did, maybe she did look like a spaceman, who might not know the rules of this place. Gary had not wanted Jessie to be there, and Jessie had seen that, but still she had stayed; she had stayed too long. When she went upstairs to use the bathroom, she went along the corridor to Eleanor's bedroom, which shared a partition wall with the guest room in which Jessie slept when she visited. Jessie remembered Eleanor's tired crying at bedtime, the sound of it coming through the wall, and then even after Eleanor fell asleep the partition wall still felt sad, as if her crying was still in there, trapped beneath the wallpaper, stuck in the wallpaper paste.

Jessie was starving. Her mother had always disliked her saying that. 'You're not starving,' she would say. 'You're just hungry.' So Jessie was just hungry, and that was easily solved. Leaving her travel bag in the hallway, she went into the kitchen, dropped Mrs Moffat's mail into the recycling bin, and took a portion of shepherd's pie out of the freezer. She liked to cook. She found it soothing – the chopping, chopping, softening, boiling down. She cooked more food than she could possibly eat on her own; she made enough to feed a family. What she could not eat, she froze. In her freezer, she had weeks' worth – perhaps months' worth – of shepherd's pie and chilli; she had about a square foot of lasagne, in individual portions, which she took out, one at a time. She blasted them in the microwave.

The dog was at her legs, whining, pawing. 'Not yet,' Jessie said. She would feed the dog after she had taken it out for its walk, and she would take it out for its walk after she had eaten.

While she was waiting for the microwave to beep, she took the kettle to the sink, and while she was waiting for the kettle to fill, she saw the crack, a hairline crack, in one of the window panes. She touched it. She could not really feel anything, any gap or misalignment, but she could see it. Perhaps it had been there for a while and had just gone unnoticed. Or perhaps the crack was fresh. Perhaps a child had kicked a ball against her window. The broken pane would have to be replaced.

She made a cup of tea in her Silver Jubilee mug. She vividly remembered the day of the jubilee. She had been ten years old, and she and all the other primary school children had been in a parade. They walked in pairs, wearing the colours of the Union

Jack and cardboard crowns with boiled sweets or jelly sweets stuck on for jewels. They waved little flags on sticks. And she had been given a Silver Jubilee mug, which she had looked after now for nearly forty years and out of which tea always tasted better.

She drank her tea and ate her portion of shepherd's pie at the kitchen table, and when she had finished, and had washed up her few things, she took the dog out. Sometimes she walked it along the track that passed the top of the street, where the trains used to run, but more often she walked it down to the river, as she did now even though it was dark, letting it off its lead on the stony shore.

The dog really belonged to Will. She wondered if it still missed Kirstin, if it ever thought of her. She remembered when she was first dating Will and the two of them were walking hand in hand through town and the dog got terribly excited when it found this woman who fussed it and spoke briefly to Will and did not look at Jessie. When they walked on, Jessie asked Will who she was, and Will said, 'She's my wife.' They were separated, he said, but – as Jessie turned to look at the woman in the navy coat who was walking away, the dog on its lead straining after her – still living together.

In those days, Jessie had never known how to refer to Will: she could not say boyfriend because he was not a boy, but one did not say manfriend. She had never liked the formality, the primness, of partner. He was her lover but she could not introduce him to people as her lover, a term which she always felt forced into people's heads an image of the two of them loving one another, the two of them naked just as clearly as if these people had been standing at the foot of the bed while she and her lover were making out. That's what it was called in the books she had read as a teenager when, directly after Enid Blyton, she had discovered Judy Bloom. Jessie had liked being married, not least because it enabled her to refer to Will as her husband, which was so much simpler. Now, if he had once been her lover, he had become her ex-lover. Her ex: how sad that sounded. They were not yet divorced but that would have to come next: she would be divorced. She had looked the word up in the thesaurus: she would be split; she would be ruptured.

The dog accepted her, but you could tell that it was hankering after Will. When he moved in with Jessie and brought the dog with him, he told her that Kirstin would not look after it. Now he had left the dog behind, but how did he know that Jessie would look after it? The note she had found that morning in January said only that he was going, not where he was going, but presumably he was somewhere he could not easily keep a dog.

He had given the dog the most ridiculous name. It was called The Four Horsemen of the Apocalypse. Before Will left, Jessie had never had to take the dog out on her own – either Will had done the dog-walking or the two of them had taken the dog out together. She had never heard him call out the dog's name in public; all he had to do was whistle and the dog would come to his side. Jessie could not whistle properly, not in that same sharp way; she always sounded as if she were beginning some tune. So she had to call out the dog's name, except that she could not bring herself to do it. She had thought about changing the dog's name, but that seemed wrong – the dog was old and would have been confused; it would most likely not respond to a name that was not its own. So she did not change its name but she did compromise:

on morning and evening walks, when the dog – a beagle, a scent hound – had gone into the undergrowth or into the water, when Jessie had had enough and wanted to go home, she would call out just 'The Four Horsemen', and no more than twice. 'The Four Horsemen!' she would shout. 'The Four Horsemen!' She felt like a fool.

No one would have known, she thought, standing there on the bank, looking at the river, that the water had come so high, overwhelming the flood defences, the river bursting its banks. The flooding had been nearly a year ago, although it felt much more recent than that. The ground on which she was standing now had been underwater: dry land had become riverbed; even carpeted interiors had become riverbed, sludgy underfoot. She had seen a Land Rover that had gone through the front of a house. The outside came insistently in. Some people had evacuated their homes; others had stayed. Jessie's house was some way from the river, but she had kept a wary eye on the situation.

It was raining now, and she had not brought an umbrella out with her. 'Never mind,' she said, and then glanced around to see if anyone had heard her talking to herself. There was no one nearby. Even the dog had gone out of sight. She could see people further away, some trying to get out of the rain, some not. If you just stayed out in it, you got used to it. Once you were soaked through, you could not get any wetter; it began to feel like one's natural medium.

She felt tired, though, and ready to get home. She tried to see the dog, and called out, 'The Four Horsemen!' Her first call was never loud enough; she made the second one louder: 'The Four Horsemen!' The loudness made it sound desperate. The dog came running. It seemed to understand that she would not call its name a third time. It did come when it was called, she did appreciate that. They walked home together.

In the hallway, she rubbed The Four Horsemen of the Apocalypse down with a towel. 'There you are,' she said. 'That's better, isn't it?' She put a bowl of dog food and a bowl of cat food down on the kitchen floor. The cat would slink out later, from whatever nook or cranny it had found.

Locking and bolting the front door, she thought of her Paul, when he would have been about two years old, or perhaps much less than that, more like eighteen months – a handful of months could make such a big difference. All she was really sure about was that in this memory of him he had been of walking age and suddenly able to reach door handles. One moment, babies could not even roll, and then they did: you would leave the room and return to find that they were no longer where they had been and it was a terrible shock; or they rolled right off the bed and onto the floor with a thud and a scream. One moment, they could not open the front door, and then they could, they did. She remembered standing in the kitchen, looking at the hallway, thinking that something was different, something about the quality of the light in the hallway was different; she remembered going to the kitchen doorway and seeing that the front door was standing wide open.

She remembered Eleanor running away from home. First thing in the morning, while her mum and dad were still sleeping, Eleanor had unlocked the kitchen door. She ran away to the bottom of the garden and stayed there, in a den that she had made in a hedge. When her parents woke up, there was panic, before they looked into the garden and saw Eleanor's legs where the hedge did not quite hide her. They made coffee to drink while they waited for her to come home, which she did as soon as she got hungry. She was home in time for breakfast.

Jessie picked up her travel bag and climbed the stairs. Halfway up, she smelt death, the terrible stink of something that the cat had caught and brought into the house to torture and kill. Even after those little creatures were dead, the cat continued to play with them as if they were still alive in some way. She would have to find the source of the smell, some little rodent body, its tiny teeth rather long and sharp; she would have to find it and throw it out, or the smell would get worse, and quickly. Even the thought of it, even the word – *rodent*, a nibbling and gnawing breed of mammal – turned her stomach.

Usually, she found the little bodies under the bed: they were either terribly soft and limp, or gone hard. One, found far too late, had been crawling with maggots. But perhaps the worst was one that felt more firmly rounded than the others – it had a certain weight – and she had felt horribly sure that it must have been pregnant. She had a dread of picking up a mouse – carefully with a piece of tissue – and seeing it twitch. They never did though. When she thought about the possibility of ghosts, she had to think of all those tiny mouse ghosts that might be in the house, accumulating under the bed.

Although the cat never seemed to bother eating the mice, Jessie had witnessed it eating a bird. It must even have eaten the beak, and the legs and feet, because all she found afterwards was some down, left like crumbs.

Occasionally, she managed to separate the cat from mice that were still alive. When these mice ran off, Jessie never saw them again. Perhaps they went to live in the walls. Did they really do that, did they live behind the skirting boards, or was that just in cartoons?

The door to the spare room was standing open. Jessie preferred it closed. She used the room for storage. She pulled the door to.

The house felt terribly cold. All year, she had been discovering things that she could not access because Will had left them password protected. When she had tried to watch their programme on television, she realised that it was inside a package that required a password that she did not know. Trying to switch on the heating, she had found that she could not: it asked for a pin code and she did not know the pin code. She had thought to herself that she would have to look through the manuals in the kitchen drawer, or she would have to phone one of those numbers that kept you on hold, one of those numbers with no humans on the other end of the line. She still had not done so though; she had managed without.

In bed, with The Four Horsemen of the Apocalypse weighing down her legs, Jessie checked her phone. She looked at her phone too much, as if she were expecting some message, which did not come. She needed to make more of an effort to stay in touch with her parents. She needed to phone them; she needed to see them. They had moved into sheltered accommodation that Jessie had not yet visited. Gail had told her about it in one of her postcards, sent after the New Year's Eve party.

She regretted going to that party, at the end of which Gary had found her asleep on Eleanor's bed, on top of the covers. 'Lying drunk on Eleanor's bed,' she heard him say to Gail. 'The dirt from her shoes on Eleanor's blanket.' Jessie had not known that she had any dirt on her shoes, her new silver party

47

shoes, until she got it all over Eleanor's comfort blanket. Jessie had rather liked the idea of being a weightless spaceman, but she was not: she was a hundred and twenty pounds of flesh and bone, pulled by gravity to Eleanor's bed, with mud on her soles. The blanket would have needed dry-cleaning. She ought to have offered to pay for it; she had not thought of that at the time.

When Jessie had said to Gail, some days later, 'I shouldn't have come,' Gail had looked surprised.

'I thought you had a nice time,' she said. 'I thought the party went well.'

'Gary didn't want me there,' said Jessie. 'He was furious with me for falling asleep on Eleanor's bed. He said I was drunk.'

'Well,' said Gail, 'you *were* drunk. You were certainly drunk when you fell into the bath.'

'When I *what?*' said Jessie.

'It's fine,' said Gail. 'It was a party.'

'But I didn't *do* that,' insisted Jessie.

'You did,' said Gail. 'And then you fell asleep on Eleanor's bed.'

Will had not been at the party with her; nor had he been at home when she got back to Hawick the next day. She had not known that he was going to be out, that he was going to be away overnight. She said to him later, 'What if I hadn't come home? What if I hadn't been here to take the dog out?'

'But you did come home,' he said, 'you were here.'

'It's your dog, Will,' she told him, 'it's your responsibility.' But even while she was saying this, he was, she seemed to remember, walking away from her, leaving the room; she was talking to his back. She supposed that really she had already

48

lost him by then, even though it was more than a week before he actually went. The note he left behind was not written on paper and placed where one might expect to find such a note, next to the kettle or tucked into the fruit bowl; he wrote it with a finger in shower steam on the bathroom mirror. He would have known that she would rise at seven and see it before it disappeared, or at least that she would see it eventually, when she had her own hot shower. She supposed it was thoughtful: he would have known that she would see a message left in the bathroom before one left in the kitchen, so she would spend less time wondering where he was, at least in theory: in fact, all these months later, she was still wondering where he was. Or perhaps he had just been unable to find a pen.

She imagined if, instead of just finding him gone, she'd had to watch him leave, how much that would hurt, saying to him, 'How will I know where you are?' and him replying, 'I don't suppose you will.'

For a long time, she had expected to see him walking through the door, coming into the hallway, but she no longer did. The dog did though: it did not seem to realise or accept that Will had gone for good, had just gone off and left them. She had told the dog – sometimes looking into its doggy eyes and speaking to it gently, and sometimes speaking sharply as she passed it in the hallway – but still it did not realise. It thought Will was going to come back. Every time someone came to the door, the dog thought that it was Will coming home. 'It's not Will,' said Jessie. 'Will's gone.' But the dog did not understand; all it heard was 'Will . . . Will . . .' It wagged its tail and watched the door.

Now she had to get used to being Jessie Noon again. She

could have kept Will's name of course, the same way she was keeping the dog's, but she had gone rather resignedly back to Noon. She could hardly bear to write it though, and did not like to see it; she could not see it without thinking of it hand-written on police statements and printed in the newspapers.

She shifted, stretched out, taking up some of Will's side of the bed as well. The cat would come up later. It would sleep at her feet, or she might wake in the night with the weight of it on her stomach, or she would feel its fur against her face in the dark.

She scrolled through her phone numbers. Will was not in there. He did not have a mobile phone. 'We *have* a phone,' he used to say, meaning the landline. 'And if I'm out of the house, maybe I don't want to be contacted.'

'For emergencies, though,' she had said, but she knew that he hated these shrill and insistent little devices that could find you in the middle of nowhere and disturb your peace.

The number she had for her parents was a landline number. It might be wrong now that they had moved, now that they were in their sheltered accommodation. They would have cords to pull if anything was wrong; someone would come running. She hoped that they were happy there, and that they would be able to stay there.

She picked up her D. H. Lawrence biography. Now he was leaving England behind and eloping with Frieda, who was leaving her children behind. Lawrence belonged to the same generation as Lenore's son, who had emigrated as soon as he could, with plans to begin a new life in a new place, but who had died in his forties from alcoholism. Jessie wondered if he ever wrote home, or ever visited. She imagined her great-great-grandmother, living in this same house in Hawick more than a hundred years ago, waiting for word of her only son.

Her eyes strayed from her book to a crack at the top of the wall, just where it met the ceiling. The crack ran along the wall as far as the door, where it veered down and disappeared under the doorframe, heading out into the hallway. Or perhaps it had started out there and was coming in. She imagined the crack like a river, carving a route through the house. When she switched off the light, she could not see the crack, but of course it was still there.

Even though Jessie often did not fall asleep until the small hours, it was not unusual for her to find herself wide awake again earlier than she needed to be or wanted to be and unable to get back to sleep. Then she might get up and start cooking, making meals that she could freeze in batches to eat in the future.

She had been preparing some cod for a fish pie when she heard a report on the radio about the languages fish spoke, and about how the oceans were becoming so noisy that the fish were having trouble communicating. Jessie finished preparing the cod and made the pie and froze it. It was still in the freezer, untouched.

On this particular morning, though, Jessie was sound asleep when her radio came on at the same time as an alarm elsewhere was going off. She woke with her heart racing, not understanding what was happening or what she had to do to make it stop. After climbing out of her warm bed, she traced the beeping to her travel bag, to the travel alarm clock that was lying buried in amongst the clothes that she had not yet unpacked. She switched it off and unpacked her bag while she listened to *On Your Farm*. Growing up in the suburbs, she'd had a longing, simultaneously, for city or countryside, either and both, anything but the suburbs, which were in between and neither. She wanted to live in the middle of London, her mental image of which was Piccadilly Circus, and to be in nightclubs at four o'clock in the morning; or she wanted a farm, to watch her crops growing, to watch her cows grazing. In Hawick, she was neither in a city nor on a farm, but every Sunday she caught the end of *On Your Farm*, and sometimes she found it satisfying, and sometimes it was just a reminder of what she did not have, of how she had thought she might live, a reminder that she still lived in neither one place nor the other.

She put her dirty clothes into the wicker laundry basket. The dress that she had worn to the conference and had left lying on the floor would need dry-cleaning. She saw that the hem was coming down; it wanted mending. She picked up her name tag and thought of the man who had stopped her outside the cafe in Carlisle, the man who had said her name, the man who knew her.

She took the name tag into the bathroom and dropped it into the bin. It was a pedal bin that was far too small, ridiculously small. When she pressed down on the pedal, the metal lid hit the wall, clanging like a gong. For something so little it was terribly loud. Every now and again she moved the bin away from the wall, but it always found its way back. Like the rug beside her bed, it seemed to creep when she wasn't looking.

She took a shower, dried and straightened her hair, and dressed. She put on a Christmas jumper; she thought it must be hard to feel miserable in a Christmas jumper. The cat and the dog were following her around; they were hungry. Jessie went out onto the landing. The door to the spare room was standing open. She could see the light of the rising sun flooding in, the shadow of the fringed lightshade bleeding down the wall. She pulled the door to.

She let the animals go down the stairs first, so that she would not trip over them. Now that she lived alone, and seeing as she worked at home, and given that she spoke only occasionally to her family, she did sometimes imagine dying in some sudden and unnecessary way – perhaps tripping over the cat at the top of the stairs and landing broken-necked at the bottom – and nobody knowing for weeks. The neighbours or the postman would notice a smell, and after a while someone would come in and find her lying at the foot of the stairs, and in the meantime the cat would have been eating her face. She did not know about the dog, whether it would try to intervene or whether it would just join in.

In the kitchen, she made herself a cup of tea and a fruit salad. She hoped, with this sliced banana, this chopped apple, this quartered plum, these brightly coloured fruits, to keep cancer at bay. Noel Edmonds seemed to believe that cancer was caused by negative thoughts, but in that case, too, a banana could help – she had read that bananas contained serotonin, which could give one feelings of happiness and well-being.

While she ate her breakfast, she began on the little stack of Christmas cards that she had to write and send. She hated the feeling of being late, of being so late with her Christmas cards that they might not arrive in time. She had been getting earlier and earlier with them. If she could get them out before December, she thought, she would be happy. Inside her parents' card, she added a note to say that she hoped they had settled in well, and that she would visit soon. Gail had given her their new address.

When Jessie had finished writing her cards, had sealed them in their envelopes and stuck on the Christmas stamps, she walked The Four Horsemen of the Apocalypse down to the postbox, and then down to the river where the dog could run free. The post would not go today – there was no collection on a Sunday – but at least the cards were in the box and would go first thing in the morning. She had known a boy at school who posted lit matches into postboxes, and ice poles on hot days, and anything else that might do damage. It horrified Jessie, to think of all that mail that might never be received, and the sender might never know.

She could not send a card to Paul, so she texted him instead. She knew it would annoy him to receive a text saying 'Merry Christmas' in November, but she sent it anyway. She signed off as 'Mum' even though when he was a teenager he had taken to calling her 'Jessie'; instead of saying 'Mum' and 'Dad' he had said 'Jessie' and 'Brendan'. Jessie's parents had not liked that; they said it was disrespectful. 'I called my father "Sir",' said her dad. Paul, in the end, called his father 'Tosser', and his mother 'Bitch', and then left.

She did not know if he actually got her texts; she did not know if he still had the same phone, the same number, but she continued to send him her greetings, her news including changes of address, and her love. No one ever replied. Every Christmas, Will said, 'Nothing from Paul?' 'Nothing,' said Jessie, but she appreciated that he asked, that he never forgot. Will had always hoped to meet Paul. He had very much wanted a child and did not seem to mind that this child was not his own. He was not a child any more though. Paul had left home before Jessie's move to Hawick; he would be thirty now. Jessie had also expected to have a child with Will, but none had appeared – that was how Will put it when people asked: *We would have liked a child, but one never appeared.* He said this, she had noticed, in the past tense. At least she had Paul, at least in a sense.

Isla knew that Paul existed – it had come up in the early days, when Alasdair was small and Jessie had sometimes looked after him – but after a while she had stopped asking about him; she had also quite quickly stopped asking Jessie to look after Alasdair. Jessie had committed the crime of giving Alasdair cola after school, and Isla had asked her very nicely not to, and then less nicely when Jessie did it again. 'You'll rot his teeth,' said Isla.

'I used to give it to Paul,' said Jessie, though perhaps not quite so young.

She was glad, later, that Isla had not pointed out that Jessie had not seen Paul's teeth for years and would not know if they had rotted.


On Sundays, Jessie liked to be busy in the garden, and then on Monday mornings she would ache from the hours spent hunched over digging out weeds.

On this cold Sunday afternoon, she raked the leaves off the damp grass, and pruned the leafless shrubs, not entirely sure that this was the right time of year for pruning and, when she stood back and looked at the trimmed forsythia, suspecting that she had been overzealous. She moved the most fragile pot plants so that they would be sheltered when the frost came. She looked around, but at this time of year there was not much more that she could do, and besides, the light would soon be going.

She went inside, put on some music, and sat down with a bottle of wine and her favourite glass, looking out of the window and listening to the King Creosote album *From Scotland With Love*, the soundtrack to a film documenting past lives - the lives of her grandparents' and great-grandparents' generations - although, as the singer-songwriter had said, you had to remember that for them it was not the past; they were in the present, at the cutting edge of time.

By the time the album had reached the instrumental reprise of 'Something To Believe In', it had grown dark outside; she was gazing at her own reflection, at her unsmiling face and her Christmas jumper. She rinsed out the wine bottle and went upstairs, closing the door to the spare room as she passed.

On Monday, on her doormat, she found her first Christmas card of the year, from her mother. Jessie had read an essay by Mark Twain in which he discussed what he called mental telegraphy, expressing his conviction - his great discovery - that thinking of a person and deciding to write to them would prompt them simultaneously to write to you; one could unwittingly read the thoughts of someone hundreds or thousands of miles away. Jessie wished it really were possible, by sitting down to write to someone, to make them get in touch with you.

The truth was, her mother also liked to get her Christmas cards out early. Inside the card, her mother had written a note about a piece of sky that Jessie's dad was missing, the final piece of a jigsaw puzzle that he had been working on before their move into sheltered accommodation. There was always so much sky in these jigsaw puzzles, so much sea, and such tiny pieces that were so easily lost. Jessie remembered from childhood how a missing piece could create a mood around the house, and whilst they might ask if he had found it yet – that edge piece, that little bit of background, that piece that was needed to fill the hole right in the middle of the picture – they already knew the answer, because of the mood in the house. *It has really upset him,* her mother had written. *We can't think where it has gone. He's hoping that it may yet turn up. It's a corner piece.*

Jessie knew the feeling herself; she lost small things too: she had lost her locket, and her turquoise earrings, the ones that went so well with her best blouse. She also lost not-so-small things: she had lost the dog's favourite tennis ball, and her new jar of marmalade, amongst other things.

She put the Christmas card on the living room mantelpiece. It was a silver star, handmade – her mother had always made Christmas cards and birthday cards with Jessie and Gail when they were girls, and she continued to do so now even without a child to keep busy. She collected anything that could be used – scraps of card and paper, the brown paper and tissue paper in which purchases were wrapped or packed, scraps of material, shiny bits and pieces that she stashed like a magpie. She had boxes full of these odds and ends, and Jessie was pleased to see that they must have gone with her to the sheltered accommodation.

The silver star looked rather beautiful against the blue of the wall, even if at the same time it looked, this star that had tumbled to earth, rather sad.

Isla said that these walls were turquoise, but Jessie thought of turquoise as green and of these walls as blue. 'Turquoise is greeny blue,' said Isla, 'like your walls.' But these walls – Jessie could see with her own eyes – were blue. It was not only the living room: this blue was the overwhelming colour of the house's interior – the paintwork, the soft furnishings, the bedding.

She had once painted a bedroom tangerine, when she was married to Brendan and studying part-time at university. It was to be the baby's bedroom, Paul's bedroom. Brendan said it would do her head in, and it certainly was vivid and rather relentless on the eye. She had done all four walls; there was even matching gloss on the skirting boards. When Brendan looked at it, he said, 'What were you thinking?' There were mice in that house too: she found mouse droppings in the kitchen cupboards, and she heard something small moving around at night, rustling in the rubbish bin in the tangerine room while she sat in the dark feeding Paul.

She would have to get a Christmas tree. Will had always been the one to go out and find a tree, and Jessie had been the one to hoover up the dead needles that it dropped. Perhaps this year she would get an artificial one, which could be kept in storage in between Christmases; it could be kept in the spare room. She knew someone who left the decorations on their tree from one year to another – the star on top, the baubles and the tinsel, everything. They just covered the tree with a sheet and brought it out each winter. It would look like a ghost, thought Jessie; it would look like the kind of ghost that a child would be if they were dressing up. Jessie would not like that: she would not like to see it, or to have to try not to see it, every time she went into the spare room, or every time she looked into the spare room as she reached for the handle to close the door.

# 1985

T HE CAMPSITE IN Belgium was full of children who
spoke French and German and Dutch, languages Eleanor
did not speak, but she seemed to understand these children
well enough to play hide-and-seek with them. At the age of
four, Eleanor had been no good at the game: her feet would
be visible, she would fidget too much, she would show her
face when she peeked; she was easily caught. But by five, she
had become an expert hider. When Jessie played with her,
she always had to shout out, *I give in!* Gail and Gary had
to shout out as well: *I give in!* And still Eleanor would not
come out. Her parents' voices would rise in pitch – *You can
come out now, Eleanor, you've won!* – so that you could hear
the slight shake, the touch of desperation. *You win, Eleanor,
please come out now!*

One afternoon, in Belgium, the other children had all
gone off to the swimming pool without finding her, and
the grown-ups had to find her instead. And a day or two
later, when she had once again been playing with the children, Eleanor had come back to the grown-ups to say that
she had been hiding for ages and no one had discovered her
hiding place; so much time had gone by and no one had
found her and she'd become frightened. The four of them
were playing a game of Happy Families when Gail said to
her, 'You did tell the other children that you were going to
stop playing, didn't you? You didn't just wander off?' 'I did

tell them,' said Eleanor, but her face took on a guilty, shifty look.

Eleanor, with her reddish hair, looked very much like Jessie; she looked more like Jessie than like Gail, like Jessie's own child might look if she were ever to have one. At bedtime, Jessie took Eleanor to the campsite facilities, where they brushed their teeth side-by-side in the mirror, their mouths foaming like the bicarbonate-of-soda volcanoes that Eleanor had learnt to make at a summer playscheme. Jessie had big front teeth – slightly crooked, *like gravestones*, a boy had once said – next to which Eleanor's looked tiny.

When Eleanor kissed her aunt goodnight, Jessie could still feel, on Eleanor's lips, the cold from the cold tap; Eleanor's mouth felt like something that had come out of the fridge.

They slept in a four-person tent. During the night, Jessie was woken by Eleanor talking. The first time, Eleanor said, 'Where's the front door?' and Jessie said, 'What do you mean? We're in a tent. Had you forgotten we were in the tent? Do you need the toilet?' She switched on her torch and saw then that Eleanor was fast asleep. She switched her torch off again and lay awake listening to the walls of the tent shifting. Later, she was disturbed again: in the dark, she heard Eleanor say, 'I've not had my fish and chips.' And even though Jessie was almost certain, this time, that Eleanor was fast asleep, she still asked her very quietly, 'Are you hungry?' In the morning, Jessie said to Eleanor, 'You talk in your sleep.' Eleanor wanted to know what she said in her sleep, so Jessie told her. 'I've not had my fish and chips? What would I say that for?' said Eleanor, as if this nonsense were Jessie's rather than her own, as if the finger ought to be pointing at Jessie for hearing such a thing in the night, rather than at Eleanor for allegedly saying it. Eleanor's parents had not heard her say anything in her sleep. Thereafter, each morning, Eleanor would ask Jessie, 'Did I talk in my sleep?' and if Jessie had heard anything she would tell her, though more often than not she had to say that she had heard nothing, and that disappointed them both.

When Eleanor had a secret, it was generally Jessie in whom she chose to confide. When, at the campsite, she lost a small toy, a new toy that had been bought for her on the ferry, it was to Jessie that Eleanor came. 'Daddy will be furious,' she whispered. And Jessie whispered back: 'Don't worry, we'll find it.' The toy was a little rubber action figure. 'Where did you last see it?' asked Jessie, and when Eleanor wasn't sure, Jessie went through everything she could think of: 'Did you have it when you went to the . . . Did you maybe leave it in the . . .' But it wasn't anywhere they looked, anywhere they could think of, and in the end Jessie had to tell Gary that it had been lost. 'But Jessie said we'll find it,' added Eleanor, who never called her 'Aunty'; she called her 'Jessie', as if she were a friend, as if she were not a grown-up in charge.

'What did you tell her that for?' said Gary. 'What if you can't?' And indeed Jessie could not find it. In the end, they had to leave the campsite without it; they had to leave with Eleanor crying her heart out. Even as they drove away, Jessie was scanning the ground – the mown grass, the dirt road – looking for that little rubber action figure. She wondered how long it would take for it to perish.

To make up for the loss, Jessie gave Eleanor her locket. Eleanor was very fond of her aunt's locket, and Jessie told her that she could wear it all the way home. She distinctly remembered telling Eleanor that she could wear it all the way home but that then she would need it back, and yet when they arrived back at Gail and Gary's house and Jessie asked for her locket, Eleanor did not want to give it to her. She made a terrible fuss and began to cry.

'I suppose you could keep it,' said Jessie, 'for one night. But in the morning, when I go, I'll need to take it with me.'

This made Gary angry. 'You said she could have it until we got home,' he said, 'and now we're home and she must give it back. Give it back, Eleanor. Give the locket back to Jessie.' There was a dreadful scene, at the end of which the locket was back in Jessie's possession and everybody was angry or upset.

When it was time for Eleanor to go up to bed, she came and found Jessie and whispered in her ear, 'When you die, can I have your locket?' But her whispering was actually rather loud, and was overheard by her father, who told her off. He sent her away to bed, but Jessie went up later and found her still awake and said, 'Yes, when I die, you can have my locket.' In the morning, over the breakfast table, Eleanor said to Jessie, 'When do you think you will die?'

Eleanor was fond of small, shiny things, precious and semi-precious things. She admired Jessie's gold watch, so Jessie bought Eleanor a watch of her own, a child's watch with all the numbers on it to help her learn to tell the time, though Eleanor continued to covet the watch that her aunt wore. She liked Jessie's earrings as well. At eighteen, Jessie did not have her ears pierced, but she did own a pair of earrings, picked out of jewellery that her mother had inherited. 'I don't need them,' her mother had said. 'I don't have pierced ears.'

'Nor does Jessie,' said Gail, who was older and did have pierced ears and who desperately wanted the pair of turquoise earrings that Jessie had got, but Jessie would not give them up. Jessie put them in a jewellery box in a drawer in her bedroom, but she suspected that Gail came in to look for them, so she moved them around, making them harder and harder to find, and sometimes she could not recall where she had put them, and lost them for months at a time.

'But can I have them,' said Eleanor, 'when you're dead?'

# TRANSLATION

IT'S A LONG *way home, and it's not an easy journey. Sometimes I stop where I am for days at a time, and sometimes I wonder about just staying there, wherever I am. I'm getting closer though, and Jessie knows I'm coming.*

J ESSIE TOOK HER second cup of tea of the day, in her Silver Jubilee mug, up to her desk, above which were shelves full of translated fiction. She had various versions of *The Outsider*, the Camus novel whose first line was so famous, so often quoted, and yet which changed from one English translation to the next; it was different in each one of her three Penguins. What ought to be stable shifted. But if a text was not allowed to rest, the responsibility could not be laid entirely at the translator's door; a text could be changed after publication by the author or an editor at the publishing house. Between one edition and another, words could change and disappear; punctuation could come and go. Although one talked about this novel and that novel, there were all these versions. It was even, perhaps especially, possible for the text to change – and to alter significantly – after the author's death, as *Ulysses* had, decades after Joyce went to his grave, and they were rewriting Enid Blyton, nearly fifty years after her death. Was anything final? She would once have said death, death was final, but she was no longer sure about that.

Just this month, she had discovered, through the radio, that the *Epic of Gilgamesh*, which she had thought to be almost literally set in stone, existed in different versions. Clay tablets telling this four-thousand-year-old tale had been unearthed in the nineteenth century, but it turned out that this was just one version, the earliest version, and most of the tablets were missing anyway. The tablets had been taken to the British Museum, but even then they could not be translated until the script could be deciphered. It must have been a long process, solving the jigsaw puzzle of those clay tablets, and with crucial pieces lost. A later version, hundreds of years younger but also incomplete, began, so she understood: 'He who saw the deep' or 'He who sees the unknown', but when she looked for it online she found yet another translation.

Jessie's most recently completed translation project was a novella, which had now been published, but she was not sure that anyone at all had bought the translation. She had not seen it in any bookshops, although she did look. She had not seen it reviewed anywhere, nor even rated online. All those months of fretting over this word or that word, deliberating over this or that turn of phrase, had been for no one but herself. She was reminded of the complicated dishes that her mother used to put together on special occasions, the hours devoted to fancy concoctions that no one had really wanted. For Jessie, in childhood, the real treats had been in tins: alphabet soup, or spaghetti hoops, which were like alphabet pasta but just the Os, the language of ghosts.

Now, she was translating a collection of short stories, some of which she found rather painful to read. In the first story, a woman begins a conversation with an unnamed man in an unnamed country immediately before he is knocked down by a car. He spends the rest of the story in a coma, while the woman visits him and imagines the life they might have together. When, at the end of the story, the woman is on the verge of accepting that there will not be a relationship between them, when she is poised to leave the hospital room for the final time, abandoning the man to his coma, it is not at all clear whether she really will walk away or whether, pausing and looking back, she will give in and return. Jessie had put the question to the author, who might eventually reply and who would no doubt say that not knowing was the whole point.

Another story was about a prize-winning photographer who is invited to an artist's studio to have his portrait painted. 'Bring your camera,' says the artist, so the photographer takes his camera and goes to the address that the artist has given him, and when he gets there he knocks on the door. The artist has pinned a note to his door asking the photographer to let himself in, asking him to take photographs of what he finds there. What he is expected to find and document is the artist's suicide. But the photographer is knocking at a different door, because the artist has given the photographer the wrong address, or because the photographer has written down the wrong address. Whoever's fault it is, the photographer is half a mile away, knocking and ringing and wondering why no one is answering, knocking and ringing, before eventually turning around and going home.

In each of the stories – not only in these two but in all of them – there was a failure to connect, and the endings seemed to hang in the air; they were barely endings at all. She did not know the writer; they had never met. Jessie had sent her a number of emails containing various queries about the work, but she had not heard back.

There were a number of ghost stories as well. In one, a child was seen falling into a well, night after night. That was the thing about ghosts: she had heard someone on the radio saying that the ghost of a monk did not just go up the stairs and disappear through the wall – it did it over and over and over again. Sometimes, Jessie thought that she liked the ghost stories the best – she had read them the most – and at other times she could not bear them. She wanted the ghosts to find peace, but they did not.

Jessie had her office in the little room between her bedroom and the spare room. It was neither well heated nor well sound-proofed, but it seemed the best choice. She had read that it was a bad idea to have one's desk in the same room as one's bed because then work and sleep became entangled, making it hard to switch off at night. When she brought her work into her bed late at night, she did so guiltily and, when she then could not sleep, she knew that it was her own fault. She could not work in the spare room, which could get awfully cold, and – perhaps even more distracting than the sudden drops in temperature and the draughts that could give you a stiff neck – there were the noises. She was not sure where they came from. She supposed it was Isla banging about next door; the houses, though solidly built, were adjoining. On the other hand, when, one evening, Jessie heard what sounded like someone shifting around upstairs, Isla was with Jessie in the kitchen. Jessie knew that Isla had heard it too when she asked if Jessie had someone staying in her spare room. 'Or is that someone in your own bed, Jessie?' she asked, nudging an elbow into Jessie's side. 'Is that a man you've got up there?'

'It's not a man,' replied Jessie, her eyes on the ceiling, as if she might be able to see right through it. 'I don't have visitors. I always thought it might be you making that noise, the sound coming through the wall, you know.'

'It must be Andy,' said Isla.

'Yes,' said Jessie.

'Otherwise you've got a ghost!' said Isla.

Jessie laughed and said, 'Yes, I think so!'

Some weeks after that visit, sitting at Isla's kitchen table, surrounded by the comforting smell of home baking, Jessie said to Isla, 'I wanted to ask you about the elderly lady who lived in my house before me.'

'Mrs Moffat,' said Isla, opening the oven to check on her rock cakes.

'That's right,' said Jessie, who had dealt with Mrs Moffat's daughter over the sale of the house. She had been aware of the homeowner's age - she had wondered whether she was perhaps the same woman she had seen at the sash window the day they drove home from Loch Ness - but she had not asked the question that had occurred to her, only now asking Isla, 'Did she die in the house?'

'Not at all,' said Isla, as if it were a question of scale. 'Mrs Moffat went to live with her daughter in Glasgow. I spoke to her on the phone just the other day.'

'Who lived in the house before Mrs Moffat?' asked Jessie.

'I wouldn't know,' said Isla. 'Mrs Moffat was already living there when Andy and I moved in here.'

'Did she have any other children?' asked Jessie. 'Perhaps one that died in the house?'

'I don't think so,' said Isla, taking out the rock cakes and setting them down on the side. 'Perhaps it's just the birds,' she said, 'scratching about on the roof.'

'Do you hear them in your house?' asked Jessie. 'Do you hear the birds scratching on your roof?'

'No,' said Isla. 'No, I don't.' She was shifting the rock cakes from the baking tray to a cooling rack. 'Are you hungry?' she asked. 'I'll give you some of these to take away.'

Back in her own kitchen with a warm batch of Isla's rock cakes, Jessie sat thinking about Lenore, the great-great-grandmother who had been living in this house in 1891, after which the trail had gone cold. Perhaps *she* had died in the house. Jessie ate a rock cake and then put away her plate, wiped the table, swept the floor, so that there could be no crumbs that might attract mice. Then she went upstairs to work, closing the door to the spare room as she passed.

Jessie sometimes thought about slipping things into her translations, things that ought not to be there; she thought about inserting little messages of her own, to see if anyone would notice. How many people read the original text as well as the translation, or closely enough to discover such a thing?

She saw marginalia in library books - in Freud's *On Dreams* someone had written, *How is it possible for one person to interpret another person's dreams?* - and she thought, *Who are they talking to?* Then she tried it herself, leaving notes in the margins of library books, which would be read by strangers: *I'm sorry.* Sometimes, weeks or months later, she would look to see if there was any reply. Just once, underneath her message, someone had written, *Who are you?* Jessie had not replied.

She worked at her desk in the mornings. At lunchtime, she downed tools. In England, she had made regular trips to Cambridge, even after moving from the Fens to the Midlands; she always ended up at the same museum. As a child, she had been disappointed by museums, which kept the past behind glass: nothing was to be touched, not even the glass. Now, sometimes, there were signs - she had seen them in natural history museums - saying *Please touch.* In adulthood, she was a museum regular, perhaps in the same way that a pub regular might have an unhealthy habit. The staff at the museum knew her; she sometimes felt watched.

She knew every inch of the place, every detail: the exhibits, the cafe, the tiled corridors, the signposts which had little figures on them the size and shape of gingerbread men, like the gingerbread boy who got eaten up by a fox, and a gingerbread girl in a skirt. Their faces were blank. The signposts with the gingerbread figures on them pointed to the toilets, which had bright orange cubicle doors that you could see in the wall-to-wall mirror while you washed your hands. On her visits to the museum, Jessie always ended up in the gift shop, looking at the children.

She had been there with Gail and her family many times before taking Eleanor there by herself. Jessie, eighteen at the time, had had other plans that day, but she had been asked, instead, to look after Eleanor for her sister. Jessie had made a fuss about it, but she had taken her in the end, and she did like Eleanor, who was easy to be with, and Eleanor liked Jessie too, and trusted her. They'd had a nice morning.

When Jessie moved to Hawick in her thirties, she saved a fortune in museum entry fees, although hundreds of miles from home, in another country, she still could not entirely keep away; in her head, she still went to the museum, wandering its corridors at night.

It had been necessary for her to find a new afternoon routine. After eating lunch at home, she did some cleaning. She went to the swimming pool at the leisure centre, where she ploughed up and down the pool, doing a punishing hour of crawl; or she went to a class, to aerobics or Zumba, something with thumping music. While she was counting lengths or beats or steps, she did not have to think about anything else. It was the same when she was cooking, when she was chopping large quantities of vegetables or kneading dough, and she had expected that it would be the same with clay: she had started a clay-modelling course, but had not found it so beneficial. Each week, she had been working with her clay to make a face or a figure emerge, and each week she ended up squashing it back into a ball. She did not like what she produced. And anyway, she found the class difficult: it was out of town, and the tutor was so softly spoken that Jessie could hardly hear her at all. She had missed the last few classes. She thought about her lump of clay, abandoned near the art room's huge sink, though kept moist for now inside a plastic bag. If she did not go back soon, they would put it back into the clay bin, and they would not refund her fee.

In the evening, she walked up to the track or down to the river with The Four Horsemen of the Apocalypse. She threw sticks for the dog to fetch, or she threw stones into the water, or she just stood and waited until it was time to go home again. She thought about the words she needed: in the coma story, should she say *She hurt* or *She ached*? It would matter, which word she chose. Context was vital. If the author wrote *Geliebte*, Jessie had to choose whether to translate it as *sweetheart* or *lover* or *mistress*; if the author wrote *Schatten*, Jessie had to decide between *shadow* and *shade*. Her choice made a difference. Sometimes it seemed like a terrible responsibility.

Will had agreed that it was important, 'but choosing this word or that word,' he said, 'is not exactly a matter of life and death.' It could be, though, said Jessie. Look, she said, at PC Sidney Miles and Derek Bentley and 'Let him have it'; look at Eleanor and 'Stay outside'. You had to be careful.

After the walk and the evening meal, Jessie worked some more, or she read.

In her *Life of D. H. Lawrence*, Lawrence was now abroad with no desire ever to go home again, while Frieda struggled to gain access to the children she had abandoned; but Jessie could not concentrate, she did not want to keep reading. She put down her book, pulled the duvet up to her chin and tried that trick of counting to clear her mind, to help her sleep; she tried counting sheep leaping over a gate, out of their field, but that did not help at all.

# 1985

JESSIE'S BEST FRIEND Amy had a scar on her cheek that she got when Jessie accidentally tripped her up into a rock garden, and she had a scar on her shin that she got climbing up a tree to fetch down Jessie's coat which had been thrown into the higher branches by Brendan Doherty.

Amy was forever complaining about something that Brendan had done, but it was obvious to Jessie that Amy had a massive soft spot for him. In secondary school, Amy asked Brendan out and the two of them became an item, although the three of them generally went about together.

Amy and Brendan argued constantly. From time to time, they would have a really bad fight that seemed to Jessie to be the one that would split them up – they never seemed very far away from something that Amy would be unable to forgive – but they always patched things up, and they went on like that for years.

'You wouldn't give me such a hard time, would you, Jessie?' said Brendan.

'Hands off,' said Amy, snaking an arm around his waist.

When Jessie came home from the camping holiday in Belgium, she heard from Brendan that he and Amy had had their last fight, that it was finally over between them.

'I've always liked you, Jessie,' he said. The two of them were down by the river. He'd just eaten a fish supper.

'You threw my coat in a tree,' said Jessie.

'Exactly,' said Brendan. 'I threw *your* coat in a tree.'

'You used to chase me with worms on sticks.'

'If I ever had a worm on a stick,' said Brendan, 'I chased *you* with it.'

'And it's really over between you and Amy?' asked Jessie.

'It's definitely over between me and Amy,' said Brendan.

Jessie was used to cast-offs. She wore clothes and shoes that had once been her sister's. She did not mind. Sometimes they were things that she had coveted for years. Brendan moved to kiss her and she let him. She could smell the river and battered cod.

It was only afterwards, when Jessie said that she really had to get home now, that Brendan said, 'When I see her tomorrow, I'll tell her we're through.'

'Hmm?' said Jessie.

'When I see Amy, I'll tell her it's over between her and me.'

'You're still together?' said Jessie.

'Nah,' said Brendan, 'it's over. I'm telling her tomorrow.' But that, said Jessie, would be too late.

She arrived home after her curfew, in trouble, with a love bite on her neck.

Jessie tried phoning Amy first thing, but no one was answering. She was keen to speak to Amy before Brendan did, to explain the situation in her own words. She decided to walk round to Amy's house, but while she was getting ready to leave – while she was trying to disguise her love bite with make-up, a shirt collar, a scarf – Gail called Jessie at their parents' house to say that she needed Jessie to look after Eleanor for the day because she had an appointment.

Jessie said that she was on her way out, that she had been

one minute away from leaving the house. If it had not been for the love bite, she would already have been out of the door, but she could not say that; she did not want anyone to know about that. While Jessie spoke to her sister, her mother hovered in the hallway, and Jessie had to keep her body turned sideways so that her mother would not catch sight of the bruise on her neck.

Gail, on the far end of the phone line, persisted, saying, 'Take her to the museum, I'll pay.' Then her mother joined in, saying that Jessie must help her sister out.

Her mother got hold of the phone and Jessie went to the front door. With one hand on the door handle, Jessie said, 'Eleanor is not my responsibility,' but she did not leave. Reluctantly, ungraciously, she gave in. She tried again to call Amy, but Amy, she knew, was already on her way to meet Brendan.

As they approached the museum, Jessie said to Eleanor, 'Can you hear that?'

Eleanor listened. 'Hear what?' she said.

'A yellowhammer,' said Jessie. 'A bird saying, "A little bit of bread and *no* cheese!"'

'I can't see it,' said Eleanor.

'No,' said Jessie, who could not see it either, 'but can you hear it? "A little bit of bread and *no* cheese!"'

Eleanor listened.

'There it is again,' said Jessie, and they listened together to the bird twitting and trilling.

'But it isn't saying that,' said Eleanor. 'It isn't saying anything.'

'No,' said Jessie, 'but we like to think it is.'

She saw a girl with Amy's hair, and another girl with Amy's jacket. She passed a place where she and Amy sometimes met, but there was no one there.

Turning back to Eleanor, she found the little girl walking in the gutter. She looked like a stray urchin, as if one of the orphans from *Annie* had wandered away from the set: her socks were sliding down her legs, and her knees were smudged with dirt; her cardigan was hanging off her shoulders. The cardigan used for the reconstruction would be almost identical; the little girl would look so much like Eleanor. Jessie heard the ding of a bicycle bell and the pip of a car horn. She fetched Eleanor back onto the pavement. Amy had noticed that Eleanor could be careless around roads. 'You need to teach her how to stay safe,' she had said. Jessie said to Eleanor, now, 'Watch out.'

Eleanor crouched down and plucked a dandelion clock from between the paving stones. She filled her lungs and blew at the seeds. 'One o'clock,' she said. She blew again. 'Two o'clock.' It made Jessie think of What's the time, Mr Wolf?, the wolf turning suddenly – 'It's dinnertime!' – and having to run so that the wolf would not catch you. Outside the museum, Eleanor took a final big breath; she left dandelion seeds on the museum steps.

One floor of the museum was given over to a series of connected exhibitions exploring ideas and images of the otherworld, the netherworld, the underworld, realms of the dead divided from our world by a boundary which, at certain times, thinned. Or they might be reached, these other worlds, via the portal of a watery place, into which offerings were sometimes cast, artefacts which might be excavated thousands of years later, pulled out of the mud.

Some of the artwork was unsettling, and Jessie said to Eleanor, 'You're not frightened, are you?'

'No,' said Eleanor. 'I'm not frightened,' but her eyes were rather wide as she scurried from exhibit to exhibit, from room to room. Eleanor would want to tell her mum what she had seen, and Gail would say, 'You'll have nightmares!' and Jessie would say, 'So will I!'

Eleanor slipped through a doorway into an exhibition of mummified bodies. She was curious about these bandaged figures – bandaged people, bandaged cats. Jessie tried to explain to Eleanor the purpose of mummification: it was to do with the dead being allowed into the afterlife, or it was to do with the dead wanting their bodies in the afterlife.

'But they're not in the afterlife,' said Eleanor. 'They're here.'

'But their spirits are in the afterlife,' said Jessie. She looked at the bodies. She could not remember how it worked, how one accessed the afterlife. It was to do, too, with the weighing of the heart, a process depicted on a nearby panel, the god Anubis checking the scales. The dead could enter the afterlife if the heart was lighter than a feather.

Eleanor scampered off again, in the direction of the cafe where they would stop for lunch, and Jessie followed, trying to keep her in sight. It had been a nice morning, but Jessie's mind was elsewhere. She was about to lose someone she loved. How easily, how quickly, it could happen.

# OUTREACH

THE JOURNEY IS *taking longer than I meant it to. I had hoped to be there by now but I'm still days away from crossing over. I've come quite a way though, and I am in more familiar territory now. I sometimes think I'll travel through the night, but once again I find myself stopping, delaying. I send another message to Jessie, and then I rest.*

THE CAT WAS obsessed with shadows. On winter mornings, the bathroom light cast a shifting puddle of shadow onto the bathroom floor around Jessie's feet. The cat followed Jessie and her puddle of shadow around the bathroom, unable to decide whether to investigate or run from this thing that it could not begin to understand. It seemed wary, and yet kept coming back to see just what it was, dabbing with a paw at the impalpable darkness. It seemed perhaps less like a puddle and more like an aura, this shadow that followed Jessie around.

As she went from the bathroom to the top of the stairs, Jessie reached down to stroke the cat between its ears. It was an odd cat. Jessie would be petting it and then suddenly it would bite, darting at her like a snake. She wondered whether it had been taken away from its mother too soon. She wondered if the mother still remembered her kitten and worried about where it had gone.

The cat turned its head and bit into the flesh at the base of Jessie's thumb, and there was just a moment of needle-sharp pain, and then the cat went on its way, trotting off down the stairs. Isla had said that Jessie ought to punish the cat when it did that, that it must not be allowed to get away with it, but Jessie would not do that. It was hardly anything, that tiny bite; it did not break the skin and barely hurt at all. And she knew that even if the cat did hurt her, she would not punish it.

Downstairs, Jessie fed the cat and the dog and herself, and then took the dog out for its walk before starting her work.

When she came downstairs at lunchtime, she found a post-card on the doormat. *I'm on my way home*, it said. 'Now you're coming,' she said to the postcard, 'after all this time.' She did not know what to do with it. In the end, she propped it up on the windowsill behind the kitchen sink, and spoke to it each time she ran the tap.

She fed the cat, but not the dog, which did not get any lunch. This was a difficult time of day for the dog, which had to watch the cat eating while it went without. Jessie refreshed the dog's water, in which it had no interest. It stood and looked at the cat eating, and then looked at Jessie, and then looked at the cat again.

She microwaved a portion of something from her freezer, not entirely sure what it was until she came to eat it. When she had eaten and washed up, she pulled the living room furniture away from the walls so that she could get behind and beneath things to clean, getting the dust balls. Under the sofa, she found one of Will's socks, with a hole in the toe.

She hoovered the stairs and the landing and the bedroom. She rarely entered the spare room, but the door was standing open and she poked the hoover over the threshold, making tracks in the carpet. The room was long and thin, and home to odd things that Jessie did not know where else to put. In the far wall, there was a sash window. To one side of it, in one corner of the room, there was a creaky wicker chair, and on the other side, in the other corner, there was a single bed which had come with the house. There had always been an expectation about this room: Will imagined there being a child in here, and so did Jessie. It was already blue, he had said, and she knew that he was picturing a boy. She pictured a girl.

The bed was old and rather uncomfortable. It was easier to keep it than to get rid of it, but it had never been used for guests. It did have bedding on it though, so it looked decent when the door was ajar, and from time to time, in the depths of the night, Jessie's insomnia brought her down the hallway to lie on this uncomfortable bed, on the dusty blanket. The room gave her strange dreams.

She was not far from the doorway when the hoover abruptly stopped, its roar dying – the plug must have pulled itself out of the wall. She could have plugged it into the socket in the spare room, but she felt that she had disturbed the room quite enough already. She retreated, winding the cord up as she left and closing the door behind her.

It was Friday. Friday had always been Jessie and Will's day for going to The Bourtree for a drink. In the months since Will had left, Jessie had continued to go without him. Sometimes she went with Isla and Andy, and when they had other plans Jessie went alone.

She ate her evening meal early, walked the dog and then filled its bowl, and the cat's. She knew that when she came home later, they would act as if they expected to be fed again, as if they had not eaten at all. She sometimes found the dog hard to live with: it seemed permanently poised between expectation and resignation, as if she were its only hope but also likely to disappoint. She wondered if the dog might have appreciated more of a routine: sometimes it had its meal and then a walk and sometimes it had a walk and then its meal; that would make it hard for the dog to know what was going to happen next, and in the meantime there was just so much waiting, so much drooling and sighing.

She changed her top and brushed her curling hair. She appraised herself in the mirror and found herself wanting but she would have to do.

At the bar of The Bourtree, she ordered a drink. She tended to drink red wine, although a few glasses were likely to leave her lips stained, and her teeth as well, which made her appear – when she saw her face in the bathroom mirror – rather ghoulish. She was watching her glass being filled when someone standing next to her said into her good ear, 'Jessie Noon.'

She looked around and saw the man who had stopped her outside the cafe bar in Carlisle, though it took her a moment to recognise him. Under the pub lights, she could see the blue of his eyes and the red in his moustache and in the beard that had not been there before. 'Hello, Robert,' she said, and she could see that he was pleased she had remembered his name. She turned around to look for her wine, which was not coming yet. She glanced back at Robert, who did not have a drink in front of him; he had his coat on, so she supposed that he had only just come in. Her glass of wine arrived just then and Jessie said to Robert, 'What will you have?'

'I'll have a pint of Abbot Ale, please,' he said.

'A pint of Abbot Ale, please,' Jessie said to the young man behind the bar.

When the pint had been set down on the bar next to the wine, Robert said, 'I'll get the next ones in.' Reaching for his drink, he said, 'You're not here with anyone?'

'No,' said Jessie.

'We can sit over there,' said Robert, picking up both of their drinks and carrying them to a booth, where they took off their coats and sat down.

'I remembered where else I'd seen you,' said Robert. 'You were at the Halloween party. You were the one with tuberculosis.'

'Yes,' she said. She remembered him now; they had spoken briefly. *It's not catching, I hope*, he had said. She had heard him perfectly well, as she did now, despite her bad ear; it must be the pitch of his voice, or the way he always turned his face towards her.

'You caught your bus all right?' asked Robert. 'After I saw you in Carlisle?'

'I did,' said Jessie, 'thank you.'

'I'd driven down, myself,' said Robert. 'But I parked somewhere I shouldn't have done. When I went back to it, the car was gone. There was just this empty space. It was a shock.'

'Yes, I can imagine,' said Jessie. 'Did you get your car back?'

'Oh aye,' said Robert, 'but it was a lot of bother, and I had to pay a fine.'

How nice that would be, thought Jessie, just to make a phone call and pay a fine and get back whatever you had lost.

'What were you doing in Carlisle?' she asked.

'My family's there,' said Robert.

'You're married?' asked Jessie.

'God, no,' said Robert. 'I mean my mum and dad, and my brothers and sisters, and *their* families, all their kids – there seem to be more every time I see them, it's overwhelming.' He gulped at his pint.

'You don't have children yourself?' asked Jessie.

'None myself,' said Robert. 'I wouldn't want them. How about you?'

'I had a child,' said Jessie, 'with my ex-husband; we had a son, but he left home years ago.'

'You have an empty nest,' said Robert.

Jessie, seeing how her reference to her ex-husband could be misinterpreted, considered explaining that she also had a husband who was merely absent, but there seemed little point; either way, she was alone in her house. 'Apart from the dog,' she said, 'and the cat.' She finished her wine. 'And I sometimes think that there might be a spirit in my house. I think it might be the spirit of a little girl.'

Robert got to his feet and picked up their empty glasses. 'Same again?' he asked.

'Yes,' said Jessie. 'Thank you.'

When Robert returned with the drinks, Jessie said, 'Do you know the Woolf story, "The Haunted House"?'

'No,' said Robert, 'I don't know it.'

'The ghosts in it are searching the house for something they left there, and what they find they left in the house is love. And that reminds me of the Scott poem, "The Eve of St John", which is set near here, in fact, near Kelso. A lady is visited by her lover, who turns out to be a ghost.'

'That must have been a shock,' said Robert.

'At *the lone midnight hour, when bad spirits have power,*' recited Jessie, '*In thy chamber will I be.* She ends up in a nunnery. And it's like "John Charrington's Wedding" by Edith Nesbit, in which the groom marries his sweetheart regardless of the fact that he's just died.'

'Does she know he's dead?' asked Robert.

'She can see that all is not well,' said Jessie. 'But I don't think she really knows until the very end. She seems to die of terror then. In Woolf's story,' she added, 'all is well. They seem to be very nice ghosts.' At that moment, she turned her head towards the bar and saw who had just arrived. She looked at his arms, forced away from his sides by his muscles. It must be uncomfortable, she thought, to carry around that much bulk. He had his back to her, but while he waited for the drink he had ordered – Jessie imagined a pint of something dark and strong – he turned his head this way and that as if looking for someone.

Robert leaned over the table towards Jessie and said, 'Are you hungry?'

Outside The Bourtree, they crossed the road to the fish and chip shop and ordered fish suppers. Music was playing behind the counter; the track that came on while they waited was a twenty-first-century remix of an Elvis Presley track whose original version Jessie had known in her youth.

A lone woman came into the shop, heard the music and began to sing along; she danced up to the counter, where she said rather breathlessly to the man who was parcelling up the fish suppers, 'They've found him, did you hear?'

'Found who?' asked the man.

'A homeless man was just found dead in New York and his dental records prove it's Elvis.'

'Is that right?' said the man. To Robert and Jessie, he said, 'Anything else?'

Robert asked for a pickled onion with his fish supper, and Jessie asked for one too. It was not something that she would normally have asked for in a fish and chip shop, although she had loved pickled onions as a child. She was not sure why she had asked for one now, just because Robert had.

'They've had him living under a witness protection

programme since 1977,' said the woman. Jessie wondered what it would be like to be one of the very few people to know something like that, to know that Elvis had never really died.

Outside, Jessie and Robert found a bench to sit on. When they opened up their fish suppers, Jessie was taken aback by the size of her pickled onion.

'It's the size of a baby's fist, that one,' said Robert. 'It'll bring tears to your eyes.'

Jessie touched her teeth to the skin, tasted the vinegar, and then found that, in fact, she could not face it.

'I'll take it off you,' said Robert. He took it and put it with his own.

They ate their fish, and Jessie was reminded of the summer she turned eighteen, of kissing Brendan by the river right after he'd had a fish supper, and afterwards, when Jessie was home again and alone in her bedroom, she had found a tiny piece of cod in her mouth.

'What work do you do?' asked Jessie.

'Social services,' said Robert.

'I imagine that's a difficult job,' said Jessie.

'It can be,' said Robert. 'A lot of people hear "Social Services" and think of someone coming to your door, wanting to take your children away, or to take you away. They think of the outreach worker coming for your loved ones, coming for you.' He picked up Jessie's pickled onion and ate it in two bites.

'I ought to be getting home,' said Jessie, folding the paper around the remains of her fish supper. Robert was just about done with his too, and they both stood and took their litter to a nearby bin.

'I'll walk you back,' said Robert.

'No,' said Jessie. 'Don't do that. I'm only a minute from my door.'

'Are you sure?' he asked.

'I'm sure,' she said. She did not set off though. They were standing near the Horse, and Jessie looked up at it, at the rider on horseback. It was a memorial to the Battle of Hornshole, a battle fought by children by the sounds of it; it had been fought to defeat English raiders and would not be overlooked or forgotten. At first, there had been only one memorial, and then, at the other end of the High Street, they had added another one. She passed these memorials every day, every time she walked to the river. Isla had told her about the battle, about the local boys and the English. She had said 'we' and 'you' and Jessie had bristled: it had been nothing to do with her; she had not even been born then.

Jessie touched the inscription on the base. She had not learnt Latin at school, and sounded it out like a child: 'Merses Profundo Pulchrior Evenit.'

'Overwhelm it in the deep,' said Robert, 'it arises more beautiful than ever.'

Jessie circled the base of the statue, running her fingers over another inscription, reading it the same way she used to read a cereal box when she was little just because it was in front of her – niacin, riboflavin, thiamin – not knowing what any of these things were even though she was eating them. 'Teribus ye Teriodin.'

'A war cry,' said Robert.

'It means "The Land of Death, the Land of Odin",' said Jessie. She had found the translation of this Old Welsh phrase in a book.

Robert said that she was wrong, that her book was wrong.

'What does it mean then?' asked Jessie.

Robert did not seem to know, but he knew that she was wrong.

They stood for a while, looking at the stone base, on which there were no more inscriptions to translate.

'I ought to get home,' said Jessie. She put her hands deep inside her pockets and said goodnight and that she had enjoyed the evening, and Robert said goodnight and that he had too. They went their separate ways without arranging to meet again. There seemed no need when they shared a haunt.

No sooner had she shut the front door behind her than the cat was at her feet. It had a tendency to appear silently out of nowhere and was almost invisible in a dark room or outside at night; she had to avoid standing on its paws or its tail. The dog had come hurrying too. They wanted their supper, though they'd already had it. Perhaps a midnight snack would do no harm, she thought, even as she eyed their thickening bellies.

Jessie went into the kitchen, with the animals at her heels. When she switched on the light, she saw her Silver Jubilee mug lying broken on the floor. She crouched down and gathered up the pieces, looking to see if it might be possible to fit them back together, to glue them in such a way that the breakage would hardly be noticeable, but some of the fragments were so small that she could see this would not work, and anyway, she would always have known. Besides, she would never have been able to drink out of it again as the cracks would attract bacteria.

She folded the shards inside a few sheets of newspaper

and placed them in the bin. Her tea would never taste the same again.

She put down food for the cat and the dog. 'What happened to my mug?' she asked them. 'Was that you? Did you knock it off the side?' But they were busy eating.

Or perhaps there had been the tiniest earthquake, which she, sitting with her drink in the pub or with her fish supper, had not noticed, but which had sent her favourite mug tumbling to the floor.

She went to the kitchen doorway and called up the stairs, 'Or was it you?' There was no answer.

The dog had finished eating and was looking at Jessie. The cat finished eating as well; it licked its lips and looked at the wall.

Jessie sat down, wondering if she wanted another drink, or if she had already had quite enough. She had only had two glasses of red wine at The Bourtree, and she'd had the fish and chips to soak it up, but she was not sure that another drink would be a good idea. She had noticed that red wine was getting stronger. It used to be something like eleven or twelve per cent but it had been slowly creeping up and now it was often fourteen per cent or more, and the glasses were larger than they used to be. She had a cup of tea instead, in a mug that she could take or leave, and she hoped that the caffeine would not be enough to interfere with her sleep.

She got into bed with her book, in which Lawrence and Frieda were living on the outskirts of England, holed up in Cornwall for the duration of the war. (Jessie thought of Eleanor growing cold in her den at the end of the garden.) The authorities watched them suspiciously; they saw the German-born Frieda up on the cliffs, telegraphing messages – so the

English supposed – to the other side, to the Germans in their submarines, when it was only her white scarf flapping in the wind, her clean laundry blowing on the line. Jessie thought of the washing she herself would peg out in the morning and imagined someone thinking that the arrangement of her pillowcases might be some kind of semaphore, might mean something more than it did. The misunderstanding was almost comical, but then the Lawrences' cottage was raided and they were told to leave.

Jessie closed the book, turned off the lamp and tried to sleep, while the wind muttered at the window and the trees shook off the last of their leaves.

# 1985

AFTER EATING THEIR sandwiches in the museum cafe – although Eleanor barely touched hers, sucking instead on her can of cola, while Jessie treated herself to a bottle of beer – they visited the toilets, following the signs with the gingerbread people on them. 'And then we'll go to the gift shop,' said Jessie.

Eleanor wanted to go into a cubicle on her own. There were three cubicles, and Eleanor chose the middle one.

'Will you be all right?' asked Jessie. 'Can you manage on your own?'

'*Yes*,' said Eleanor, closing and locking the door.

Jessie went into one of the neighbouring cubicles.

Through the cubicle wall, Eleanor said, 'Why does the door look like a fish finger?' It sounded like a joke: *I say, I say, I say, why is a door like a fish finger?* But it was not a joke; it was a serious question.

'Do you mean the cubicle door?' asked Jessie.

'Yes,' said Eleanor.

Jessie looked at it. It was orange. 'Well,' she said, 'I suppose it's because of its colour, and its shape.'

Eleanor did not reply.

'Eleanor?'

'Yes?'

'I suppose it looks like a fish finger because it's the same colour and shape as a fish finger.'

'But *why*?' said Eleanor. 'Why did they make the door look like a fish finger?'

'I expect it's just a coincidence,' said Jessie. She heard the flush of a toilet.

'What?' said Eleanor.

'I don't think it's supposed to look like a fish finger,' said Jessie. She heard the unlocking of a cubicle door. 'Is that you, Eleanor? Have you finished? Stay outside, Eleanor. Stay right by the door.'

When Jessie, adjusting her clothes, came out of her cubicle, she looked around for Eleanor and saw that the door of the cubicle that Eleanor had gone into was still closed. 'Are you still in there, Eleanor?' called Jessie. A woman was washing her hands but there was a free sink. Jessie stood next to the woman and turned on the tap. She could hear Eleanor singing quietly to herself inside the cubicle. The woman left and Jessie waited for Eleanor to come out. 'Are you all right, Eleanor?' she asked. She heard the movement of the toilet roll inside the metal holder. She heard the flush.

When the cubicle door opened, it took Jessie a moment to understand that the girl coming out of the cubicle was not Eleanor. Now all the cubicles were empty, and the only people in the room were Jessie and this strange girl.

Drying her hands on her clothes, Jessie went to the door. She was ready to tell Eleanor off, to say to her, 'I told you to wait by the door,' but, she thought, if Eleanor was waiting just outside the door – on the wrong side but still right by the door – then technically she had done as she was told.

But she was not there.

Jessie walked back down the corridor, into the body of the museum, looking behind the pillars and in the spaces where

Eleanor liked to hide. She went to the gift shop; she walked all around it but could not see Eleanor anywhere. She went to the cash desk, where the lady on the till was making small talk with a customer, and while Jessie waited she kept looking around for Eleanor. The till had an LED display that said:

| G | O | O | D | B | Y | E | | H | O | P | E |

Jessie watched as the letters shifted slowly to the left, until it read:

| | H | O | P | E | | T | O | | S | E | E |

and then:

| S | E | E | | Y | O | U | | A | G | A | I | N |

When Jessie reached the till, she asked the cashier if she had seen a little girl, five years old, on her own, looking lost, but the lady said that she had not; she said she was sorry.

# INTERCOURSE

*I* HAVE BEEN *inland for a long time, but now I am nearing water. I have left a trail of things behind me: a pair of shoes that were half a size too small and rubbed; socks that were going thin, going through; a cardigan missing buttons, although it's cold now, here. But I have what I need to complete my journey, and will be crossing soon.*

JESSIE DREAMED THAT she was by the river; she was kissing Brendan, but in the dream he was still seventeen while she was the age she was now, which was nearly fifty. She woke up feeling ashamed, with the taste of battered cod in her mouth.

It was Saturday morning, and she found herself thinking of Amy, whose father had left the house one morning as if he were going to work but who did not come home at teatime nor for years. Then, one weekend, Amy came down to breakfast and found her father sitting at the kitchen table, and her mother said, 'Your father's home,' as if he had just finished a really long shift or as if he had been out to fetch a pint of milk but from a shop on the other side of the world.

'Now I have to *hear* them,' Amy had told Jessie, 'through the wall.'

'Hear them doing what?' asked Jessie.

'You know,' said Amy. 'Through the bedroom wall.'

'Oh,' said Jessie.

She had *seen* them as well; she described something monstrous in the dark of her parents' bedroom, the incomprehensible shape of them against the wall, a single shape that was darker than the rest of the room, like a creature with two heads and a terrible tangle of limbs, moaning and groaning. 'I'm *never* going in there again,' said Amy.

Jessie had never been aware of her own parents doing any

such thing. Her dad had his thousand-piece jigsaw puzzles, and her mother had her craft projects. There was nothing to hear through the partition wall in the dead of night.

'You're glad your dad's come home though, aren't you?' asked Jessie.

'Yes,' said Amy. 'I just don't want *that* going on. They're far too old.'

*The same age I am now*, thought Jessie. She tried to think how old she and Amy would have been then, but all she was sure about was that it must have been before the summer of 1985, before Jessie started seeing Brendan, after which Amy vanished: whenever Jessie went to Amy's house, Amy was out, or so said her mother, standing in the kitchen doorway, guarding the threshold, like Anubis, thought Jessie who felt herself judged and deemed unworthy; Jessie's heart, if weighed, would be found to be heavy. Jessie was not invited in, and after a few weeks Amy had gone away anyway, to university, while Jessie had deferred her own place.

The last time Jessie knocked on Amy's door, her mother said Amy was on a gap year abroad, and she made it clear that Jessie was not to come to the door again; she was not welcome. 'I think,' said Jessie, 'Amy's got one of my singles. Would it be possible to get it back?' But Amy's mother, saying, 'Goodbye, Jessie,' closed the door. It was 'Wuthering Heights' by Kate Bush, and Jessie never did get it back.

Perhaps Amy would have been more forgiving if Jessie had not continued seeing Brendan, if she had not moved in with him, married him, had a child with him. It was more than a little salt rubbed into the wound.

Jessie had looked Amy up on Facebook, but had not tried to make contact with her. She had looked Paul up as well but he was not on there, and she already knew that she would not find Will there. Alasdair from next door was on there but he was not active; all his posts were old.

Jessie's mind was still on Amy when she heard someone knocking on the door. She pictured her childhood friend standing on the doorstep in the winter sunshine, as if Jessie had brought her there just by thinking about her. But it would not be Amy, who had not spoken to Jessie for decades now, to whom Jessie continued to send Christmas cards – care of Amy's parents who still lived in the same house, always writing her own address on the back of the envelope – but who did not reciprocate.

It would not be Paul, and it would not be Will coming home – he had a key and would not need to knock.

Thinking then of Robert, she put a hand up to her hair, which was still wild, not yet brushed let alone straightened. She had not washed. She had not even looked at her face; she might have sleep in her eyes and yesterday's eyeliner adding to the dark circles underneath them. Whoever it was knocked again, and Jessie went downstairs in her dressing gown. She opened the door and felt a mixture of relief and disappointment when she saw that it was not Robert after all.

'Come in,' she said to Isla. Jessie had not yet had her first cup of tea of the day, and whether or not she had sleep in her eyes, she did still have sleep in her head – a fuzziness, a softness, and the remnants of her dream, which she began describing to Isla: '. . . kissing him by the river,' said Jessie; 'he was only seventeen.' Isla remained in the doorway, with the door open and one hand still on the door handle. When Jessie stopped talking, Isla said, 'I was wondering if you have an egg. Alasdair wants one for his breakfast and I've none in.'

Jessie went to her fridge, found an egg and gave it to Isla; she tried to give her a couple but Isla would only take the one. She closed the door behind her.

Jessie felt the unseemliness of what she had said hanging in the air, as if, by describing her dream, she had opened some door that ought to have been kept shut; she had shown her neighbour something that ought not to be seen.

She went back upstairs and took a long shower, and then set about making a large fruit salad for her breakfast. She always felt that if she had her five-a-day first thing in the morning, she was less likely, in the rest of the day, to go too far wrong.

She sat down with her fruit salad, and wondered if she ought to buy a blender and make herself smoothies, the kind that could cleanse and detox.

She had said the word 'walk' to the dog, which it understood, and she had even taken its lead off the hook and had put some dog treats into her pocket – this was the happiest the dog would look all day – when there was another knock at the door. This time Jessie was expecting to see Isla standing there; she thought she could apologise to her for mentioning the dream which Jessie thought Isla might have found distasteful. But when Jessie opened the door, she was greeted by the postman holding post that would not go through her letter box: there was something for Will – for whom post kept arriving, a pile of it accumulating, unopened, on the kitchen counter – and a parcel for her. There were also a few envelopes, amongst which she looked for a postcard that was not there.

Inside her parcel, she found another book that wanted translating, sent by a very small publisher with distribution problems and a history of putting out work that did not sell and failed to attract any attention. She doubted that her translation would ever be read, but she rarely turned work down; it was best to keep busy. She leafed through the book and opened the envelopes, all Christmas cards. In return, she wrote some extra cards of her own, for people she hardly knew or no longer saw. There was one that needed to go abroad, and she suspected that she had already missed the last posting date.

She was used to signing for both of them – 'Jessie and Will' – and in some cases continued to do so now. Her name on its own looked insubstantial; she wished that she had bought smaller cards, with less white space to fill. She added kisses, put the cards into their envelopes and sealed the flaps.

By the time she took the dog out for its morning walk, it was almost lunchtime.

She was down by the river, throwing stones into the water – the dog running after each one even though they sank and could not be found and brought back to her – when she saw someone coming along the riverbank, a figure reminiscent of the man she had seen on the nudist beach in her childhood; or in fact, she thought, when he was somewhat closer, he looked like D. H. Lawrence, in his three-piece suit, with his red beard. Staring at him, at this figure that seemed to have come out of her childhood, out of the past, she realised that it was Robert. When she thought he was near enough to hear, she said to him, 'You look like D. H. Lawrence.'

He had seen her, but did not seem to have heard, perhaps because of the noise of his feet on the pebbles, or the noise of the river.

Raising her voice, she said, 'You look very smart. Are you going somewhere?'

'I'm just out for a walk,' he said. 'A bit of fresh air.'

'In a three-piece suit?' asked Jessie.

'Why not?' said Robert. 'My granddad wore a three-piece suit every day of his life. This was one of his; it came to me when he died.'

'I expect it would please him to know you're wearing it,' said Jessie.

'I wouldn't have thought so,' said Robert.

Jessie turned to look downstream. She called out, 'The Four Horsemen!' Robert, startled, tried to see what she seemed to be seeing. 'The Four Horsemen!' she called again, and the dog came running.

'Oh,' said Robert. 'That's the dog, is it? That's your dog?'

'It was my husband's dog,' said Jessie. 'I suppose it is mine now, yes.' She clipped the lead to the dog's collar. 'Are you walking back?' she asked, although even as she was asking the question, she was starting to walk, and Robert was walking alongside her.

'And what else do you do?' he asked. 'Other than walking your ex's dog. What are your hobbies?'

'Hobbies?' said Jessie, smiling at the question, which was the sort that one might ask of a teenage penpal.

'Aye,' said Robert. 'What does Jessie Noon do in her spare time?'

*Jessie Noon*, in the third person, as if Jessie Noon were someone else entirely. Jessie mulled this over: 'What does Jessie Noon do in her spare time?'

'Is there an echo?' said Robert.

Jessie was on the verge of saying, 'An echo?' but stopped herself. 'I work a lot,' she said. 'I'm self-employed. I work from home. I can work into the night if I want to.'

'And do you?' asked Robert.

'Sometimes,' said Jessie. 'Yes, I often do.'

As they passed the Horse, Robert said, 'And when you're not working?'

'I like to cook,' said Jessie.

'You don't look like someone who cooks,' said Robert. 'You're too thin.'

'Are you hungry?' asked Jessie.

'I'm always hungry,' said Robert.

'I can make us some lunch,' said Jessie. They walked together up the street to Jessie's front door, and Robert followed her inside. Jessie told him not to worry about his shoes, which were clean and would do no harm on her hard floors. Nonetheless, standing just inside the hallway, he unlaced his brogues and placed them neatly together near the door. There was a hole in one of his socks – his big toe was poking through – and she saw him notice it; she saw his embarrassment. She looked away so that he would not know that she had seen it.

She fed the cat, but not The Four Horsemen of the Apocalypse, who looked at her, and she said, '*You're* always hungry as well, aren't you?'

She went through the freezer, telling Robert what she had. He liked the sound of the casserole, which Jessie microwaved and brought to the table. He asked for water and she filled her favourite glass for him, but he said, as he took it from her, 'There's a crack in this,' and when she looked she saw that there was, a crack so big that she wondered how she had not noticed it and how the glass was even holding together.

It was only when they were settled and beginning on their meal that it struck Jessie that no one had sat there and eaten with her since her husband had left. The casserole was Will's favourite.

'This isn't bad,' said Robert, indicating the casserole with his fork. 'My own speciality is a curry, which you ought to try some time.'

'I'd like that,' said Jessie.

'What's your line of work?' asked Robert. 'What is it that you're doing when you're working past your bedtime?'

Jessie told him about her translation work. 'I mostly translate fiction,' she said. 'I enjoy it. I like the idea that someone will then be able to read and understand something they otherwise couldn't.' It was a mediation between languages, she said; the word 'translation', from Latin, meant something like 'bringing across'. 'It's not an exact science. The word you choose might have the right meaning but the wrong nuance; or it might have the wrong meaning – you do have to be careful. Words can be tricky.'

'Who's that?' asked Robert, looking towards the window.

Jessie turned around in her seat to see who was there. 'Oh,' she said, seeing that he was looking at a photograph propped up on the windowsill. 'That's Will, my—' She searched for the right term and found that she could not say 'ex'. 'That's my husband,' she said, 'but he's gone, he left.'

Robert nodded. Gesturing towards another photograph, he said, 'And that's your son?'

'Yes,' said Jessie. 'Who has also gone.' Paul's photograph was already old when he left. 'I have the animals to keep me company.' Sometimes the house seemed terribly quiet.

'You have a ghost,' said Robert.

Jessie cocked her head to listen for some sound, and then realised that he was only bringing up what she had told him.

She wondered if she was right to have mentioned it; perhaps such things should be kept to oneself, like the unsettling dream that she had told Isla about. Nonetheless, she said to him, 'Yes, I think I do.'

'Have you seen it?' he asked.

'No,' she said. 'I haven't seen it.' She recalled the night she and Brendan went looking for ghosts; she told Robert about it now. She did not remember whose idea it had been, to drive out to the countryside, to what had once been a convalescent home for war veterans, with a mental hospital wing. By the time she and Brendan went, it was abandoned and said to be haunted.

They had gone at night, with torches. They left the car on the main road and walked up a side road, away from the street lamps, climbing over a gate to get onto the driveway. At first they could not see to the end of the driveway, which disappeared into darkness, but as they walked, on and on towards their own torchlight, the old Victorian hospital became visible in front of them, a black slab against the moonless sky. When they got closer, they could see the ivy climbing the red brickwork and creeping over the windows.

The door was ajar: they were not the first trespassers. A sign in the window said ALL ITEMS OF VALUE HAVE BEEN REMOVED.

The floor was crunchy with plaster that had fallen from the ceiling, and with glass from the smashed windows, in whose frames only shards remained. Their torches flashed from the debris-strewn floor to the broken windows to the potholed ceiling to the walls scrawled with graffiti – YOU THINK I'M GONE!

Wheelchairs had been abandoned in the corridors, and

there was evidence of people having slept in the side rooms, perhaps for a dare.

Brendan said they should turn off their torches, so they both turned off their torches and stood there in such darkness that there might have been nothing but the small patch of ground they were standing on, the ground they could feel beneath their feet, and beyond that an abyss.

They stood at the foot of a flight of stairs, their torchlight barely touching the gloom above. 'Do you think there's anything up there?' asked Brendan.

'Let's go and see,' said Jessie, beginning to climb.

Upstairs, they found more corridors and side rooms, more abandoned equipment, more graffiti – We R not Alone. 'I think we've seen everything,' said Brendan. 'Let's go.'

When they were outside again, about to begin their walk back down the long driveway, Jessie glanced back at the building.

'I think,' she said to Robert, drawing his empty plate across the table and stacking it on top of hers, 'I was still hoping to see a ghost, to see one at the window, watching us go. There was nothing there, nothing to see, but you just got this feeling . . . And it's the same here. The spare room door won't stay shut. And I hear things. Mostly I just get this feeling . . .' She took their plates to the sink. 'Come and see for yourself.'

She led him up to the landing, where they found the spare room door standing open. 'You see?' said Jessie, eyeing the crack that sat in the angle between the hallway wall and the ceiling and stretched towards the bedroom.

'So this is the ghost's room,' said Robert, walking in.

Jessie was aware that the room appeared quite ordinary.

She stood in the doorway while Robert looked at the door and the frame and the hinges.

'What makes you suspect,' he said, 'that your ghost is a little girl?'

Jessie told him about Eleanor, about losing her at the museum.

'You *want* it to be her,' he said. 'You want her to be here.'

'I don't know,' said Jessie.

'Do you think she's here to punish you?' asked Robert, coming out onto the landing again.

'I don't know,' said Jessie, but she thought about the fissures that had appeared in the house, as if it were succumbing to some pressure or force. She thought about her favourite glass, cracked, and her special mug, broken. She felt watched, and she did not feel forgiven.

'Perhaps it's not the house that's haunted,' said Robert.

'I don't know what you mean,' said Jessie.

'There's no getting over something like that,' he said.

'Of course not,' said Jessie, closing the door behind them.

They were only a few steps from her bedroom, and the possibility of turning in that direction, of inviting Robert into her room, crossed her mind. She imagined Will coming home, and having to say to him, 'There's someone else.' She imagined Will standing in the doorway, on the doormat. 'I'm sorry,' she would say.

They walked to the stairs and went down to the hallway, where Robert put his shoes on, putting away his holey sock, his naked big toe. He thanked Jessie for the lunch, and left.

In what was left of the afternoon, Jessie did her household chores. After putting fresh covers on the bed, she sat down with some mending, listening to The Proclaimers – 'I'm

Gonna Be (500 Miles)' and 'I'm On My Way' – while she put a neat row of stitches in the hem of her wedding dress, her translation conference dress. She repaired some favourite underwear, which had been waiting on her mending pile for months. She turned up 'Sunshine On Leith' before threading a darning needle and bowing her head over the hole in the toe of Will's sock. According to the census records that Jessie had seen, her great-great-grandmother had worked weaving woollen hosiery, and Jessie liked the feeling of sitting in Lenore's house darning a sock, the activity connecting her, she felt, to Lenore, the past alive somehow in the present. But while she was fixing the hole in Will's sock, she found herself thinking about the hole in Robert's.

During the week, Jessie found herself looking for Robert, looking twice at men who had his colouring, his stature, his gait, seeing doppelgängers everywhere.

She worked late into the night. She had begun the translation of the new book. There were words, phrases, images about which she would very much have liked to ask the author, but the author was long dead. Although, she considered, it was not really necessary to say *long* dead, to stress that as if it were pertinent, as if a long-dead author were somehow further away than one who was only *recently* dead, as if Jessie might still stand a chance of putting her questions to a newly dead author, as if it would just be a matter of finding the means of communication, perhaps just asking loudly enough, listening hard enough, and doing it quickly, before too much time went by.

On Friday, she went to The Bourtree, where she talked to a neighbour and another dog-walker she recognised. She saw

Kirstin, though not to speak to. She stayed later than usual, drinking more than she meant to, but she did not see Robert.

At the weekend, she made another casserole, and froze it. She did her laundry and was hanging her underwear on the line to dry in the winter daylight when Isla's back door opened and Alasdair came out. They made small talk while Jessie pegged up her pillowcases and Alasdair got to work mending a puncture on his bicycle. The bicycle was leaning against the low wall that separated their two yards, and Alasdair was crouching over a washing-up bowl, inching the inner tube around in the water, looking for the leak. When Jessie had hung up the last of her washing and had picked up her empty basket, she paused by the wall and watched him patch the hole. She was complimenting him on his hands – '. . . lovely long fingers,' she was saying, 'like a pianist; do you play?' – when she saw Isla standing at the door, watching the two of them.

Jessie smiled at her and said, 'Hello, Isla.'

'Hello, Jessie,' said Isla, but she was not smiling. 'Alasdair, come inside, please.'

'I'm mending my puncture, Mum,' said Alasdair.

'I said, come inside, please,' said Isla.

Alasdair mumbled something under his breath, but he stood up, leaving his bike and his tools where they were, and went inside with Isla, who closed the door.

Jessie took her empty basket inside and set about putting fresh linens on her bed.

On Monday morning, Jessie found another postcard on her doormat. She looked at the back, at the handful of words in Will's cramped handwriting, and at the photograph on the front, and at the postmark. 'Well,' she said, 'you're not coming very quickly, are you?' Perhaps he was not coming after all; perhaps, in between the sending and the receiving, he had changed his mind.

She put the postcard on the kitchen windowsill with the first one, and waited to see if there would be another.

She had begun the nightly process of filling her ear canal with oil, which sometimes seemed to ease the pressure and improve her hearing and sometimes seemed to make it worse, and which always caused a mess.

Trying to lie very still in bed, on her right side, she continued to read the D. H. Lawrence biography. Just now, he was in his prophet phase, claiming that we had lost touch with the cosmos, that we no longer knew how to communicate with it. Well, thought Jessie, perhaps that was so.

She woke on her back in the night. She could hear a wet sort of noise. It made her think of the Frogman, the damp slap of its feet against linoleum . . . She listened for a while before switching on the bedside lamp and looking towards the door, where the dog was lying across the threshold, licking itself. The dog looked back at her. 'It's just you, is it?' said Jessie. She switched off the lamp and after a moment the sound began again, and Jessie tried to imagine it being a Frogman after all, its wet feet slapping towards her, but now she knew it was only the dog, licking itself in the dark.

In the middle of the week, Jessie saw Robert in the frozen food aisle of Morrisons. Jessie had been looking for peas, and was just fetching a bag out of the chest freezer when she realised that the person reaching into a nearby freezer cabinet was Robert.

'Hello,' she said.

Robert looked up. He had a bag of frozen roast potatoes in his hand. 'Hello, Jessie,' he said.

'I haven't seen you all week,' said Jessie.

'I've been at St. Abbs,' he said. 'I've been diving.'

'In the sea?' said Jessie. 'In this weather? Isn't it cold?'

'Oh, it's very cold,' said Robert. 'It's worth it though. It's a different world below the surface.'

'How deep do you dive?' asked Jessie.

'I can't get down very deep at all,' said Robert. 'I have problems with my sinuses.'

'Do you go often?'

'I go when I can.'

'I think I can smell the salt on you,' said Jessie. Looking at what he was holding, she said, 'Please don't buy frozen roast potatoes.'

'I promised to make you my curry,' said Robert.

'I don't think you promised,' said Jessie, 'but if you're offering . . .'

'I am offering,' said Robert. He put the roast potatoes back into the freezer. 'Are you done?' he said to Jessie as she put the peas into her basket.

'I think I am,' said Jessie.

They went together to the checkouts, and then carried their bags through the town centre. Nearing the bottom of her street, Jessie said, 'I've got these peas that I ought to put in the freezer.'

'Put them in mine for now,' said Robert.

They walked on, until Robert turned down a dim alleyway, and Jessie hesitated for a moment. *Do I really know this man at all?* she thought. And then, even though she did not, she followed him into the alleyway, her shopping bags awkward at her sides in the narrow space. Robert unlocked a door and Jessie saw the hallway beyond: tidy, tiled, scrubbed clean.

The kitchen, too, was spick and span, with everything in its proper place and all the surfaces kept clear. 'You're very tidy,' said Jessie.

'I try to keep things in order,' said Robert, unpacking and putting away the contents of his shopping bags.

His kitchen windowsill was bare while her own was always cluttered: apart from the postcards and photographs, she had pot plants – herbs – and various odds and ends. Robert's windowsill would not get much sun, but still she said to him, 'I can give you some herbs – some coriander and some basil.'

'I don't want plants,' he said, washing his hands at the sink. He took an apron down from a hook and put it on; it was stripy, dark blue and white, like a butcher's. 'They always die.'

'Do you go away a lot?' asked Jessie.

'I like to get away,' he said. He picked up an onion and reached for a knife. Chopping the onion made him cry, and he lifted his free hand towards his face as if to rub his eyes but his fingers were oniony so instead he pressed the back of his wrist to his eyes. He looked as if he were acting in a tragedy.

'Can I do anything to help?' asked Jessie.

'You can keep me company,' said Robert, slicing into a green chilli. He cut quickly, with what seemed like no distance at all between the knife blade and his fingers. Jessie was wary of distracting him and after a minute of silence he said, 'You could put on some music.' There was an iPod, on which Jessie found the Manic Street Preachers. As the first track began, she said, 'I haven't heard this for years. This came out when my son was little.' The Manics had been Paul's favourite band.

They had listened to the music together in the living room, then later he listened to it alone, in his bedroom, turning it up louder and louder, his bedroom door vibrating, until all of a sudden he was gone and his room was silent.

Robert was pouring oil into a pan, heating it up. Jessie watched as he slid the onion and the chillies from the chopping board into the pan, and added powders and pastes, a pinch of this and a spoonful of that. Already it was smelling very good and she told him so and he smiled. 'Are you sure I can't do anything to help?' she asked.

Robert nodded. 'Wash your hands then,' he said.

He gave her a tomato to chop. She began to slice and dice it and Robert said, 'Look at your hands.' Jessie paused, mid-cut, and looked at her hands.

'I did wash them,' she said.

'No,' he said, 'I mean they're so white. Look at mine.' He held out his own hands, showing her their redness. He was still holding the wooden spoon with which he had been stirring the curry, and a drip fell onto the floor tiles. He cursed, and there was tension in his movements as he put the wooden spoon back into the pan, tore a sheet from the kitchen roll he kept to hand, and bent to wipe up the stray spot of sauce. When he had binned the stained sheet of kitchen roll, washed his hands again and returned to the chopping board, he said, 'You're bloodless.'

'I'm not,' said Jessie, though the word had many meanings. She had once been called 'cold blooded' as she stood shivering at a bus stop, wishing that she had worn a coat or at least a cardigan. She had objected to that as well; she had not liked the sound of it. She had tried to stop shivering as if to prove it, but she had been unable to.

As her knife slid through the tomato flesh, she thought of the man on the train with the plaster on his finger. She tried to be careful.

'Can you take a bit of heat?' asked Robert.

'A little bit,' said Jessie. Something she had not thought of for years came into her head and she said to Robert, 'I once set fire to the fence around our house. We had an incinerator and I lit the contents. It got out of hand and the fence burnt down. And then while the fence was missing, the tortoise escaped. We never saw it again.'

'Your tortoise ran away?'

'Yes,' said Jessie, although even she, who had been there, could not really imagine how.

'I bet you got some punishment for that,' said Robert.

'I didn't really,' said Jessie. 'I thought I would. I kept expecting it. The worst thing was waiting for it.' She remembered the awful feeling of not knowing when it would come or what form it would take. 'Perhaps they thought losing the tortoise was punishment enough.'

'Did you get another one?' asked Robert.

'No,' said Jessie. 'Another time, I set fire to our chimney. I could have burnt the house down.' That was her dad's voice inside her head: *You could have burnt the house down.*

'You want to be more careful,' said Robert, putting a lid on the saucepan and turning the flame right down.

She asked if she could use his bathroom, and he told her where it was. 'Mind yourself on the stairs,' he said. 'There's no handrail.'

Robert had a retro claw-foot bathtub, whose lion's paws reminded Jessie of a tomb she had once seen, a sarcophagus with those same feet but made of stone; she had imagined it wandering around in the night, or walking away - one morning, she had thought, there would just be a space where it had been.

On the shelf behind the bathroom sink, there was a glass bottle of perfume, its shade somewhere between blue and green, like a watercolour sea. At the same time as wondering who it belonged to, Jessie noticed a fine layer of dust on the bottle. She had never been in the habit of wearing perfume, but she tried on some of this scent, spraying some onto the pulse point of her wrist and then putting her nose close to her skin. She liked the way it smelt. Replacing the bottle on the shelf, she noticed that she had disturbed the dust on the glass; she could see where her fingers had been. She washed the perfume off with soap before going back down to the kitchen, where Robert turned and looked at her as if he had remembered something or was trying to, and she wondered if he could smell the old, turquoise perfume through the strong, rich scent of the curry that was bubbling away on the hob.

'We need to put your peas in my freezer,' he said.

When they had scraped their plates and drained their coffee cups, there was the question of what would come next. 'Do you want to . . . ?' said Robert, tipping his head in the direction of the stairs. Jessie smiled and said yes, although he could be suggesting almost anything, she thought, as she followed him upstairs; she might be agreeing to any number of things.

Kissing in a strange bedroom reminded her of her youth, of boys she did not know well enough to be getting into bed with. It was late, dark outside. She worried that Robert would want to have the light on, to see her, but he kept the light off. She thought of waking up on strange sheets, looking at strange wallpaper, and she wished that she had invited him to her house instead, although his curry had been very good. On the other hand, she might not sleep there, and then there would be no waking up wondering for a moment where she was.

There was an awkwardness to their kissing, as if it were the first time for each of them, as if they were used to not being touched. Jessie was aware of not having cleaned her teeth; she did not have her toothbrush there.

As Robert undressed her, Jessie tried, in the dark, to keep track of where her clothes were going, on which side of the bed they were being dropped. Robert, lying with some of his weight on Jessie, said, 'I'm all right like this, am I?' and Jessie, liking the pressure where their bodies touched, liking the weight of him on her, said, 'Yes.'

He was careful with her, as if he were afraid of harming her in some way, although he was not careful in the way her mother would have meant: they did not use protection; Robert went in, to use her dad's term, without his wellies on.

She did sleep, until daylight began to intrude around the edges of the blinds' wooden slats. She was facing Robert, whose eyes were closed. The duvet was down around his waist, exposing his torso; those red hands of his gripped the top edge as if someone might try to pull the duvet off him altogether.

Three-quarters of the way up his arms, his old suntan ended in a line beyond which he was pale; he looked as if he were wearing the ghost of his summer T-shirt. She ran her fingers up his arm, over slack muscles, over the line, touching him with fingers that must have been chilly, waking him up.

'Good morning,' he said, and she laughed at the formality;

it was the sort of thing one might say to the postman over the garden gate, not to someone lying naked beside you.

'Good morning,' she said in reply, her cold fingers creeping over his pallid chest, nearing his heart, nearing its pulse, but Robert was pulling away, turning away to sit up. Perched on the edge of the bed, he was gathering up his clothes, pulling them on. 'You'll want to be getting home,' he said, 'to that dog of yours. It will be wanting its breakfast, won't it? It will be wanting a walk.'

'Yes,' said Jessie, 'of course.' It would have wanted its walk and its supper last night as well, and she felt bad about that. With the duvet still covering her, she tried to reach her clothes, but in the end it was necessary to leave behind the warm den of the bed and hunt around the cold room for yesterday's underwear.

When she was dressed, she made her way from the bedroom to the kitchen, where Robert was making coffee. It was an echoey house. It was almost entirely devoid of soft furnishings. While her own house had hard floors downstairs, his had hard floors throughout. He had no curtains, just wooden blinds. He had no cushions. She supposed that the hard, bare surfaces were easier to keep clean.

As Jessie came into the kitchen, Robert reached for the iPod and put the Manics on again, a more recent album, *Everything Must Go*, and Jessie recognised 'Further Away', which she recalled seeing described as 'almost a love song'.

Jessie drank her coffee quickly, while it was still too hot. Her shopping was by the door, put there ready for her to collect as she left. Seeing her putting her shoes on and picking up her bags, Robert came to the door and held it open for her. 'I'll see you,' he said, and she echoed it back to him: 'See you.' When she was outside and walking away, he called to her, 'Take care,' before closing the door.

This, thought Jessie, was the walk of shame that one might do in one's teens, in one's twenties, but surely not, God forbid, at the age of forty-nine. Without having showered, without having combed or straightened her hair, without having brushed her teeth, she walked through the town centre, past her neighbours' houses and up to her front door with the Morrisons bags weighing her down on either side. She realised, as she let herself in, that she had left her peas behind in Robert's freezer.

She found The Four Horsemen of the Apocalypse standing in the hallway, looking at her. 'I'm so sorry,' she said. She saw the look of shame on the dog's face, and the mess behind the door. 'That's my fault as well,' she said, and she went to the dog and stroked its head and cleaned up the mess. She fed the animals and took the dog down to the river. Already it seemed to have forgotten about what had happened; it seemed happy enough anyway.

Back home, in the kitchen, Jessie saw that where there had only been a hairline crack in the windowpane, she could now see and feel the break; the two segments of glass had shifted like tectonic plates.

She made a cup of tea and settled down to work, trying to make up for the hours lost the day before. She worked through mealtimes, only snacking when she grew hungry, although she gave the dog an extra big supper and took it for an extra long walk. She worked until late and then took a hot shower and got into bed. She read a chapter, in which Lawrence mistreated a dog, and Jessie loved the book for its kindness, for how it tried to understand and forgive Lawrence for his flaws.

At the weekend, Robert drove them out to a nearby village, in the car that he had reclaimed from the compound in Carlisle. They drove with The Four Horsemen of the Apocalypse in the footwell.

Wrapped up in woollens and winter coats, they walked in the Cheviot Hills, following a track that necessitated clambering over a gate, which made Jessie feel as if she were trespassing or somehow doing something wrong.

With countryside all around her, Jessie thought of her farm; or she would like to have an animal sanctuary, a place for retired seaside donkeys and rescued battery hens. She kept the dog on its leash so as not to scare the sheep; she thought of Hardy's ewes, in *Far from the Madding Crowd*: two hundred of them, and pregnant, going over a precipice one after another, lying dead and dying in the chalk pit, their footprints left behind where the fence was broken through.

When they reached a hilltop, Robert took out his vacuum flask, poured a cup of tea and passed it to Jessie. She drank it gazing towards the border with England, which was close enough to walk to. Then Robert took the empty cup back and refilled it. He placed the cup on the grass while he screwed the top back onto the flask, but the cup tipped over and his tea spilled out. Jessie saw Robert's jaw tighten. Holding the cup so that Robert could pour the last of the tea into it, Jessie told him about a short story she had recently read, which mentioned Patsy Cline's belief in parallel universes, and that they touched one another in wet places: 'puddles, spilled milk, even bits of the body,' said Jessie. 'I don't know if it's true.' Robert was not listening or did not respond. He took the cup out of her hands, and she reached out with the pointed toe of her boot and touched the wet patch of grass.

Robert had booked a night's accommodation above a pub, and they had their evening meal there, with pints of Old Golden Hen. Robert asked Jessie about her plans for Christmas, and she told him that she had no particular plans for Christmas Day, but that afterwards - in between Christmas and New Year - she would be going to visit her parents in their sheltered accommodation, and from there she would go to her sister's house for a few days. 'At least, I think that's the plan,' she said, 'but I haven't speaken to her for a few months.' She knew something was wrong, but she could not for a moment think how to correct it. Or *was* it wrong? She tried again: 'I haven't speaken to her . . .' No, it was wrong, but she could not put it right; she could not find the word.

'You haven't spoken to her,' said Robert.

There was the word she wanted; she felt herself relax.

'Are you close to your sister?' asked Robert.

'We used to be closer,' said Jessie, 'when we were kids. I haven't seen her since the New Year. When we were little, we shared a room. We had a cupboard that scared me. It had a mirror on the front, and in the dark the mirror looked like a doorway that you could just walk through, and I imagined walking through it and not being able to come back, getting stuck in this other world, this mirror world. So Gail went into the cupboard, going behind the mirror to show me that there was nothing to be afraid of. But when she spoke to me from inside the cupboard, it sounded as if she had gone into the mirror world and was talking to me from there, calling to me. It begame . . . It begame . . .' Robert was looking at her as if she had lost the plot. She said, carefully, 'Became a game.'

She took a sip of her Old Golden Hen; she was nearing the bottom of the glass. 'I played the game with Eleanor, too, with the same cupboard, in the same house.'

'Who's Eleanor?' asked Robert. 'Oh, the girl in the museum.'

It was a strange way to put it; he made it sound like Eleanor was still in there.

'The little girl you lost,' he said, as if she might need reminding.

She finished her pint, put down the empty glass and said, 'How strong is this?'

'About four per cent,' said Robert. 'Four point one.'

It was unlikely to be the beer then, interfering with her tongue. Perhaps it was her ear, that muffled feeling, making her lose her words. Or it might be the ghost; it was hard to think straight, knowing there was something there, in the house. Robert would be thinking it was the beer. 'It's the ghost,' she said. Robert glanced around. 'It's distracting, exhausting. What do you suppose it wants? There's always something they've come back for.' She had once read a poem about a ghost that wanted its shoes. She thought about her missing jewellery.

Or perhaps it had not come back; perhaps it had always been there, following her around.

'You need a good night's sleep,' said Robert.

'Is that all?' said Jessie.

'Let's get the bill,' said Robert.

They settled the bill, left the restaurant and went up to their room. The dog stayed so close to Jessie's heels that it tripped her up on the stairs. She swore at it and it looked sorry, but then did it again.

When they opened the door to their room, the dog was eager to get through the doorway with them, and then, when it was inside the room, it was eager to get out again. It pawed at the door, and at the carpet where it went under the door. 'Come and settle down,' said Jessie, switching on a lamp and laying the dog's blanket out on the floor beside the bed. The dog lay down with a sigh and within a few minutes it was asleep. It was all that walking in the hills, thought Jessie; it was all that fresh air. But she had done the same amount of walking; she'd had the same amount of fresh air: she wished that she could fall asleep like that.

Going to the window – approaching her own reflection, which seemed to be on the outside, looking in – she closed the curtains. They took turns in the bathroom and undressed self-consciously before getting under the duvet, where Jessie reached for Robert, who, as he reached for the switch to turn off the lamp, told her that her hands were cold. She blew on them and rubbed them together to warm them up; it reminded her of being out in the snow, her extremities going numb.

Later, when she was lying awake in the dark, with voices from the bar coming through the floorboards and drifting up the stairs, she found it soothing to listen to The Four Horsemen of the Apocalypse breathing softly, and when it whimpered and twitched in its sleep as if it were having a bad dream she reached down and stroked its soft forehead and hoped that it would know she was there.

# 1985

'YOU QUEUED?' SHOUTED Gary. 'You bloody queued?'

The police queried this too: 'You queued?' they said. 'You queued in the gift shop, before telling anyone that Eleanor was lost? How long did you queue for?'

'I don't know,' said Jessie. 'Probably not as long as it seemed.'

The first few hours were crucial, she knew that. But the hours passed.

The police kept coming back, to see if she had remembered anything else, to see if her story had changed. They kept asking her what she had said to Eleanor before she went missing. 'I told her to stay outside,' said Jessie.

'Outside the bathroom?'

'I meant outside the cubicles,' said Jessie. 'I told her to stay right by the door.'

'Which door? The cubicle door?'

'The bathroom door, I suppose,' said Jessie.

'You told her to stay outside the bathroom door?'

'I said outside,' said Jessie, 'but I meant, inside the bathroom, by the door.'

'But that's not what you said.'

'No,' said Jessie, though she hardly knew any more.

'And what time was that?'

'I don't know,' said Jessie. 'It was after lunch. We'd had

lunch. I wasn't wearing my watch. I'd not been able to find it that morning. I think Eleanor had taken it.'

Gary was standing in the living room doorway with his arms folded; he looked like a bouncer. 'Eleanor was wearing her own watch,' he said. Eleanor's watch, her learning-to-tell-the-time watch, would be found outside the museum.

'You're wearing a watch now,' said the officer.

'I found it later,' said Jessie, 'in Eleanor's bedroom.' It had not been wound and had stopped.

'What were you doing in Eleanor's bedroom?' asked Gary.

'I was looking for my watch,' said Jessie.

'So, after you lost Eleanor,' said Gary – he was speaking slowly and carefully, as if he were picking his way through a foreign language – 'you went into her bedroom to look for your watch.' Jessie could not meet his gaze; she saw the tendons in his neck, and the white of his knuckles.

Jessie's mum came out of the kitchen; she offered tea and asked Gary to come and help her. He could be heard banging cupboard doors while the questions continued.

'And you said you spoke to Eleanor *after* that?' said the officer. 'After she left the bathroom?'

'I *thought* I was speaking to her,' said Jessie. 'I thought she was still inside the cubicle. I asked her if she was all right.'

'But she wasn't still inside the cubicle?'

'No,' said Jessie.

'So you weren't talking to her after all.'

'No.'

The officer said, 'When you realised Eleanor was not in the bathroom, what did you do?'

'I finished washing my hands . . .' began Jessie.

'You finished washing your hands?'

'I finished washing my hands and left the bathroom,' said Jessie. 'I thought Eleanor would be just outside. But she wasn't. So I walked round to the gift shop.'

'You walked?'

'Yes,' said Jessie.

'You weren't hurrying?'

'No,' said Jessie. She ought to have run, like a greyhound let out of its box. She always felt so sorry for those skinny greyhounds, so thin they might just snap, pelting after a hare that they could never ever catch.

'So you walked to the gift shop, where you queued. And when you got to the front of the queue . . .'

She had been thinking that at any moment she would see her, that Eleanor would suddenly come into view or appear at her side, wanting something. Jessie remembered the till's scrolling LED display: GOODBYE HOPE TO SEE YOU AGAIN GOODBYE . . . 'I said I'd lost a little girl,' said Jessie.

'Was anyone with you in the bathroom?'

'There was a lady standing at the sinks,' said Jessie.

'And what did this lady look like?' asked the officer, poised to note down these vital details.

'I don't know,' said Jessie. 'I wasn't really looking at her.'

'Will you try to remember?' asked the officer.

She did try. For years, at night, she had been seeing the blur of her in the mirror, this figure who never came into focus.

# COMMUNION

IN BRUGES, A woman in a bar asks me where I've travelled from. I tell her. 'But that's not where you're from,' she says; she asks me what I was doing there.

'I'm not sure,' I say. 'I just ended up there.'

'And what are you doing here?'

'I'm just passing through,' I say. 'I'm on my way home.'

She notices my wedding ring. She asks me if I have children.

I tell her I don't. I tell her I was always hopeful but that a child never appeared.

She laughs. 'Poof!' she says, making a gesture with her hands suggestive of a magic trick, of something appearing or disappearing in a puff of smoke. And then, more seriously, she says, 'If you want a child, you'd better hurry home.' She pretends to shoo me out of the bar as if there is no time to lose. 'Go home,' she says.

I stay, though, for a while. I like the beer they have here; I like the Grimbergen.

I go to an art gallery and to a cathedral. I find myself at the edge of a tour conducted in a foreign language, understanding only odd words and disembodied phrases, deciphering fragments – 'und der Organist'. When two women pass me, I think I hear, in amongst a wash of language I cannot comprehend, 'Kim Kardashian'.

IN THE MORNING, there was no hot water – there was a problem with the boiler – and Jessie was persuaded to leave her shower until she got home. Robert was keen to get back to Hawick in time for church, for the Sunday service.

'Which church do you go to?' asked Jessie, when they were on the road.

'I've tried them all,' said Robert. 'I'll go to the mid-morning service at the Congregational Church.'

'I've wondered about going in there,' said Jessie. 'I keep walking past.'

'You could come with me,' said Robert.

'I don't know,' said Jessie. 'I've not had a shower.' She did not want to enter the church for the first time smelling of sex. 'And I've got the dog. I ought to take the dog for a walk.'

He dropped her off outside her house. Jessie put her travel bag inside her hallway and then walked the dog down to the river.

The dog waded into the water. Jessie, standing on the stony riverbank, breathed deeply, filling her lungs with the fresh, cold air. She loved the river. She closed her eyes and listened to the water rushing by. She thought of Robert sitting in a church pew, singing his heart out and praying to a god she found it hard to believe in.

When she opened her eyes, the dog had disappeared. 'The Four Horsemen!' she shouted. 'The Four Horsemen!' The dog came running through the water, splashing Jessie's unwashed legs. 'Good dog,' she said, touching its head. 'Good dog.'

She walked home with the dog at her heels. Closing the front door behind her, she thought she heard someone inside the house. She moved further into the hallway, which was colder than ever. She called out, 'Hello?' She went to the stairs and called up them, 'Hello?' She could hear the scratching, but other than that there was no sound, no reply.

In the kitchen, she found a corner of her window missing, glass smashed in the sink. It was too small a hole to have been used for trespass, though she did check for intruders – she found the spare room door ajar and closed it as she passed, and on her bedroom carpet she found down feathers that resembled dandelion seeds – before returning to the kitchen window to make a cardboard barricade.

The dog was looking expectant. 'You've already had your breakfast,' she told it. She supposed it had forgotten. She fed the ravenous cat, while the dog watched with its tongue hanging out.

Jessie collected her travel bag from the hallway and took it upstairs. She was feeling uneasy. She had yet to do the laundry that she normally did on a Saturday, and the gardening that she liked to get done on Sundays: there was no growth to speak of but there were leaves – dead, damp – accumulating on the grass, and there was algae climbing the walls. She had not even washed and now it was almost lunchtime; she was behind.

She stripped the bed and carried the laundry basket downstairs with the dog at her ankles.

The bedding was still damp on the line when she took the

dog out for its bedtime walk. As she paused in the yard to finger her pillowcases, she saw Alasdair attempting to mend another puncture, or the same one, with only the light from his kitchen window to see by. She called hello to him over the little wall and would have stopped for a chat, but his reply was mumbled and he would not look at her. He went inside and closed the door.

Down by the river, throwing sticks and stones for the dog in the dark, she managed to put both her feet in the water, both her boots, which were not in the least bit waterproof. She squelched home and had a hot bath before getting into bed.

She was nearing the end of the Lawrence biography. When she put in her bookmark, when she laid the volume on her bedside table, she knew that very soon Lawrence would die, and she could feel the sadness of it coming.

During the week, she caught Alasdair in the yard a couple of times and tried to ask him whether he would look after the dog and the cat for a few days after Christmas, while she was away in Cambridgeshire, but on the first occasion he sloped off on his bicycle before she had got the question out, and on the second occasion he slunk into the house without speaking to her, while she called after him, 'I'll pay you!'

When she saw Isla, she asked her if Alasdair was all right; she said she'd been hoping to talk to him.

'What do you want with Alasdair?' asked Isla.

Jessie, surprised by Isla's tone, said, 'I was hoping he'd look after the animals when I go away after Christmas.'

'He can't,' said Isla.

'Is he going away?' asked Jessie.

'No,' said Isla. 'He's not going anywhere.'

'I will pay him,' said Jessie.

'He's not going to do it any more,' said Isla. 'Please don't ask him again. Don't text him. Don't Skype him. Don't poke him on Facebook.'

Jessie was still standing on her side of the wall with her mouth open when Isla went inside and shut the door.

Back in her own living room, turning on the lamp that brought the shadows to the wall above the mantelpiece, Jessie found herself unbearably chilly. She put on a cardigan. She wanted to tell Will what Isla had said; she wanted to tell him about this terrible misunderstanding. She picked up her phone and composed a text to Robert but did not send it.

The cardigan was not enough. She thought of the blanket on the bed in the spare room; she could fetch it out of there and wear it like a shawl; it would be a dusty comforter. She left the blanket where it was though, and went to bed early instead.

She read her book. She turned a page and Lawrence died, far from home.

On Friday, she met Robert in The Bourtree.

'I like your blouse,' he said, as they sat down. 'That's a lovely blue.'

Jessie looked down at it and said, 'It's turquoise.' It was the one that matched her favourite earrings. In her ears, she had simple silver hoops, which she did not especially like. She was not even sure that she liked having pierced ears; it sometimes seemed like an odd thing to have had done to her lobes, to have given them those unnecessary little holes, those unnecessary little scars. The piercing of her ears had been a present from Will. 'Now you'll be able to wear your heirlooms,' he had said. And she had; she had taken the turquoise earrings out of safekeeping, and had worn them along with the locket, and then lost them. She had misplaced her wedding ring as well now, though she could not remember taking it off.

'Do you know that man?' asked Robert. He nodded towards the bar and the figure whose bulky arms did not touch his sides.

'Yes,' said Jessie, only now realising that she had been watching him. He was standing in his usual spot, looking around like he was searching for someone.

As if her awareness of him had drawn his attention, he turned fully and saw her and made his way over. He was carrying his drink, a half pint of cider, it looked like; the little glass looked comically small in his hand.

'Evening, Jessie,' he said.

'Good evening, Stewart,' said Jessie. 'Can I get you a drink?' Even though he already had a drink, she could not help offering; she would have liked him to accept one.

'No, thank you,' said Stewart, holding up his little glass of cider.

'Would you like to sit down?' asked Jessie, patting the padded seat beside her.

'No, thank you,' said Stewart. 'I won't intrude. I just wanted to say hello.'

'Is there any news?' she asked.

'No,' said Stewart. He paused as if he wished there were more to say, something to add, and then he moved away, with his drink in his hand, returning to the bar.

'Who was that?' asked Robert.

Jessie finished her wine and put her empty glass down next to his. 'That was Stewart,' she said. 'His son walked into the path of an oncoming train. He had his earphones in and was looking at his phone. Stewart had just sent him a text message. The train was being driven by my husband, Will. It happened last year, although Stewart always says it seems like yesterday. Stewart's son is in a coma.' She had heard that they were talking, now, about turning off his life-support system.

They both looked at Stewart, sipping his cider and watching the door.

'Will stopped working after that,' said Jessie. She had sometimes thought that it was just as well that trains no longer ran along the top of their street. But after decades of dormancy, trains were once again running on the Waverley Line, and although they currently stopped short of Hawick, Jessie did not doubt that the track would be extended, the trains would reach them, sooner or later; they would hear them and perhaps even feel them in their house.

'Will became like a shadow of himself,' she said. 'He was just waiting, all day, every day, for news of Stewart's son, whose condition never changed. I couldn't reach him. It was like he'd shut a door between us. He was absent long before he left.'

'How long has he been gone?' asked Robert.

'Since January,' said Jessie.

'Almost a year, then,' he said.

'Yes.'

'It's Christmas on Sunday,' he added.

'So it is.'

Robert picked up their empty glasses, took them to the bar and came back with fresh drinks, and Jessie said to him, 'How would you like to come to my house for your Christmas dinner?'

'That's very kind,' said Robert. 'On Christmas morning, I'll be at church. You could join me.'

'I'll be busy with the dinner,' said Jessie.

'We can eat later,' said Robert. 'We can cook together after church.'

But Jessie said no, she would want to start cooking in the morning. 'There'll be a service on the radio,' she said. 'I'll listen to that in the kitchen.'

'It's not the same as being there,' said Robert.

'I'll go some other time,' said Jessie.

She would be glad to have someone to cook for, a reason to peel the potatoes and trim the sprouts and cut the little crosses in the stalks; a reason to roll out the pastry and cut the perfect circles and grease the holes in the pie tin. She did not think she would have cooked a Christmas dinner just for herself; she would have microwaved a portion of something from the freezer.

'Shall I bring anything?' asked Robert.

'Bring my peas from your freezer,' said Jessie.

On Christmas Day, after the morning service, Robert arrived on Jessie's doorstep with a bottle of red wine, which he handed over, and a gift wrapped in Christmas paper, which he kept with him while he took off his shoes. He showed Jessie his socks: 'New Christmas socks,' he said.

'Very nice,' said Jessie.

He took off his coat, showing Jessie his jumper: 'New Christmas jumper,' he said. She admired it, and Robert, in turn, admired hers. 'I'll put your present under the Christmas tree,' he said, moving towards the living room.

'There isn't a Christmas tree,' said Jessie.

'Well that's no good,' said Robert.

But she had switched on the fairy lights that hung from the gas light fixtures, and she had put some antlers on the dog.

'Do you not think that's cruel?' asked Robert, looking at the dog.

'He wears them every year,' said Jessie.

'That doesn't make it all right,' said Robert. 'I bet you hate Christmas, don't you?' he said to the dog. 'Here.' He handed Jessie her present, and she produced one for him. Beneath layers of shiny wrapping paper and tissue, Jessie found a bottle of the turquoise perfume. 'I noticed you wear it,' said Robert. Jessie thanked him, and he carefully peeled the paper off his own gift, finding a little box much like the kind an engagement ring might come in. When he opened the lid, he found cufflinks inside, plain silver squares, on which, said Jessie, he could have something engraved. 'You could have a favourite line of poetry,' she said, 'or a line from a song, or anything you like.' She ought to have had them engraved before giving them to him, but there had not really been time, and she would not have known what to ask for.

'Thank you,' said Robert. 'I love them.'

Jessie opened the wine he had brought, and handed him a glass. He took a sip. 'That's good,' he said, and he raised his glass to the dinner that Jessie was making. He eyed the various dishes and pans and said, 'I forgot the peas.'

'It doesn't matter,' said Jessie. 'Everything else is ready now anyway. We'll manage without the peas.'

She turned off the radio and put on some music. While Jessie laid the table, Cass Elliot sang 'Does Anybody Love You', and, as Jessie sat down with Robert, 'Make Your Own Kind of Music', which now reminded Jessie of *Lost*, which she had watched with Will, all six seasons, over six years of her life, and she still wasn't really sure what had happened; she had been left with a sense of confusion and disappointment.

When they finished the first bottle of wine, they opened a second one, which Jessie had bought, but it was not as good as Robert's and he told her so.

'It's all right,' said Jessie.

'It's *all right*,' agreed Robert.

After their Christmas pudding, they watched *It's a Wonderful Life*, which Robert had never seen before. 'How can you not have seen it?' said Jessie. 'It's a classic. I watch it every year.'

'What if it's not on?' asked Robert.

'It's always on,' said Jessie. 'But I've got the DVD so I can watch it anyway, whenever I want.'

He did not see how she could watch the same film so many times. 'You know what's going to happen,' he said.

'Shush,' said Jessie, and turned up the sound.

They ate the mince pies and the Christmas biscuits and opened a box of chocolates, and when the film finished Robert said, 'I've eaten too much.'

'Me too,' said Jessie.

'I do this every year,' groaned Robert.

'Me too.'

'I'm never eating again,' said Robert.

'What are you doing in between now and New Year?' asked Jessie.

'I'll be around,' said Robert. 'I'm going to a buffet on Wednesday. You can come with me if you like.'

'That's the day I'm going home,' said Jessie, 'to see my

parents and my sister. I need someone to look after the dog and the cat,' she added, looking questioningly at Robert.

'I can come round and walk the dog and feed them,' said Robert, 'if you give me a key.'

'I have a key I can give you now,' said Jessie, rising from the sofa with difficulty, her belly so full of mince pies and other goodies that it was rounded. She raised the hem of her Christmas jumper to show him: 'I look pregnant!' she said.

'Don't even say that,' said Robert. 'That's the last thing we want.'

# 1985

JESSIE WISHED THAT she had not said anything about drinking a beer in the museum cafe.

'You were drinking?' yelled Gary. 'While you were supposed to be looking after Eleanor?'

'It was only one beer,' said Jessie. 'You can drive after one beer.'

'That doesn't make it right,' said Gary. 'Your reaction time . . .' He raised his hands, made a gesture of disgust, and left the room without finishing his sentence.

There had not been much progress since Eleanor's watch had been found. There had been nothing, really, but dead ends. But they never stopped expecting to see her; they never stopped listening out for a little hand knocking at the door, or little feet coming into the hallway. If Eleanor was walking all the way home, it would take her days, especially if she walked slowly, if she walked very slowly, if she needed to stop and rest – she would need to stop and rest – on her way home. 'She always walks slowly,' said Gail: she walked painfully slowly; she messed around, taking fairy footsteps, stopping to balance on one leg, walking backwards, holding her breath.

Jessie still saw Eleanor's name in the papers from time to time, along with her own, though less and less now. Life carried on, and in a way that was the worst thing.

She moved out of her parents' house and into a cheap flat in another county. She married Brendan and took his name.

# VISITATION

I WAKE IN *my hotel room in Bruges to find that I have been bitten, perhaps by something that flew into the room or perhaps by bed bugs; I have been bitten terribly in my sleep.*

*I keep finding bumps, tight bumps that itch. I try not to scratch them while I eat my breakfast. I try not to scratch them while I travel on towards the Channel where I will cross. They keep coming up, these bumps, more and more of them, or perhaps I am only just noticing them all. I worry that I might be somehow bringing the bed bugs – or whatever it was that bit me – home with me. Perhaps I will carry them into our bedroom; I will find my own bedsheets infested.*

*I cross from Belgium into France. When I was a boy, I always wanted stamps in my passport; I wanted a record of where I had been. Now I like the way it feels to cross a border without documentation, without the thud of an ink stamp; I like to slip through unobserved.*

*I approach the ferry terminal in Calais. When I was here with Jessie, we could see the camp from the road: the tightly packed tents on the far side of the mesh fence. Now, the camp is gone; I don't know where they are, the thousands of migrants who had to disperse. The army, in camouflage with big black guns strapped across their bodies, looked in through the windows of our car and through the windows of all the vehicles that rolled by.*

Now, here again without Jessie, I'm a foot passenger, with very little luggage, walking onto the boat that will take me home.

IN THE LULL between Christmas and New Year, Jessie packed her travel bag ready for her journey south. She stripped the bed, even though it was not the weekend: she would sleep on fresh sheets and go home to her family feeling clean. She put the bedding into the laundry basket and carried it down to the washing machine. When she had emptied the bedding into the machine, she found, right at the bottom of the wicker basket, the missing piece of sky, the missing corner of her dad's jigsaw puzzle. She could not think how it had got there. It hardly seemed possible that she should find it just there, when it had last been seen in the childhood home she had rarely visited since leaving; and how many times had she emptied her laundry basket in the meantime? And yet there it was, down at the bottom of the basket, wedged in the weave, a bit of blue sky. She put it into her travel bag, into a little pocket where it would be safe.

She took the dog for a longer walk than usual, and came back past the fish and chip shop, stopping to get herself a fish supper: battered cod, without the pickled onion. She ate it back at home, sitting at her kitchen table, eyeing the windows, looking for any new cracks. She finished an open bottle of wine, not wanting to waste it.

After locking up, she went upstairs, pulling the spare room door to as she passed on her way to the bathroom. She soaked for a while in a hot bath and then got into bed, in between the layers of clean cotton, and tried to sleep.

Awake in the night, she listened to the thumping and scurrying that might have been the cat chasing after a mouse, and the wet slapping sound that was probably just the dog licking its private parts. She was regretting the fish supper, which was lying rather heavily on her stomach. But what was really keeping her awake, she decided, was that creaking sound and, faintly, a knocking sound, coming from the spare room.

She got out of bed and, in the dark, made her way out onto the landing, where she stood and looked at the spare room door, which was ajar. Will had always referred to the house as settling, or trying to settle: it must have been trying to settle for decades, from one century to the next.

She pushed the door a little further open. The room, with its parted curtains, was moonlit; the blue carpet looked like undisturbed water.

'Eleanor?' she said. She glimpsed something, felt the faintest touch of something against her leg. She looked to see if the cat was darting away down the hallway, but it was too dark to tell.

When she stepped forward over the threshold, when her foot touched the carpet, she almost expected to see ripples. She crossed the room slowly, carefully, making her way to the far end, to the bed, where she sat down.

'Eleanor?' she said.

She saw The Four Horsemen of the Apocalypse standing in the doorway, watching her. She clicked her fingers, but the dog did not come. She said its name, but it did not come. In the privacy of their house, in the dim room, she used its full name, but it did not come.

Jessie lay down on the narrow bed, on which she was a little bit cramped. She watched the darkness, while the sash window trembled in its frame.

When she woke in the morning, it was after seven. The radio had come on in her own room, and she had not heard it.

She had wanted to leave the house early, but she also wanted to have her shower and straighten her hair and have her five-a-day for breakfast, so that she would feel all right on the journey. She wanted to wear her watch, and spent some time looking for it but could not find it.

She had meant to catch a bus before eight o'clock and to be at her parents' house that afternoon, but in the end the bus she caught left well after eight and her plan went to pieces. It was gone ten by the time she reached Carlisle: she had missed the train she'd had her eye on and would not leave Carlisle now until after eleven; she would not reach her parents' house until the evening. Her mother would put out a tea at five o'clock, but she would wait for Jessie to arrive before starting to eat; the tea would spoil. Even though Jessie would call ahead to warn her mother that she would be late, still at five o'clock her mother would put out the tea because that was teatime, that had always been teatime, and they would wait for her, terribly quietly, with the inherited retirement carriage clock ticking, ticking. Her mother would say that she had done it on purpose: *perhaps not consciously*, she would say, *but subconsciously you wanted to miss that train.*

Killing time in Carlisle, Jessie had a cup of tea in the same cafe bar that she had been to previously. She found herself watching the entrance, looking for Robert, who did not appear.

Someone said, 'Look what you've gone and done,' and Jessie turned to see the spilt juice, and a child sitting looking at it, so sorry but not knowing what to do about it, other than wanting to touch it, as it spread across the table.

Jessie kept reaching for her travel bag to make sure that it was still there, patting the side pocket in which she had put the piece of sky that was to be returned to her dad.

She caught the late morning train. She favoured the route that had only one change, minimising the likelihood of her missing a connection. She would change at Birmingham New Street. There had been sinkholes in Birmingham, and elsewhere. She had seen them on the news: giant sinkholes in roads and driveways and gardens. Something shifted beneath the surface, and then the ground just collapsed; you went to step outside your door, or you came down the same road you always came down, and found that, where there had been solid ground, there was just a vast hole.

From Birmingham, the train headed vaguely east. As if dithering, procrastinating, it veered up to Leicester before turning towards Cambridge again. When Jessie had moved with Brendan to the Midlands, Gail had promised to visit her, and she had kept her promise. Jessie had gone to meet Gail's train at Loughborough station. As the train from Leicester pulled in, Jessie stood on the platform scanning the carriages, looking for a familiar face through the orange doors' long windows, not entirely sure that her sister really would be there, that when the doors opened, her sister would step out, would come forward and hug her. She still could not quite believe that Eleanor would not be there.

Normally, they would have gone to a museum. Gail had been a history student and had always loved museums. She had included Jessie in National Trust excursions; she had family membership. But now, Jessie did not like to suggest it, and was left not knowing quite what to do.

Recently, Jessie had been to Leicester Cathedral to see Richard III. When she had first heard the news about this king, whose remains had been missing for centuries before being found beneath a council car park, she had had to think which one he was: he was the bad one, she decided, the one who had locked those two young princes in the Tower of London, those two boys who had then disappeared. She did not know exactly what the king had done, the extent to which he had been responsible for the disappearance of those children, but he was generally thought to have done something wrong. Now his bones had come up. They had found the boys as well: workmen had found two small human skeletons in a box in the keep. In Leicester Cathedral, Jessie saw the king's brand new tomb, which, she read in the promotional material, was made out of fossil stone: *Within it are long-dead creatures immortalised now in stone.* A crucifix was carved into the tomb, cut deep to *allow light to flood through it, symbolising that death is not the end.* In the gift shop, she bought a postcard to keep.

One museum to which she always meant to go but to which she never had been was the National Justice Museum in Nottingham. It was possible to see, in this museum of crime and punishment, such things as a victim's bathtub ('I don't know why you'd want to see where she died,' said Gail), a cell door, and the gibbet irons used to display the condemned while they died of thirst, or to display them even after execution. *An eye for an eye and a tooth for a tooth,* thought

Jessie. One of these days, perhaps on her way home, she would go.

In Cambridge, she caught a bus, which took her deep into the Fens, where it was so flat, where you could see for miles, though not everywhere of course; in a city, for example, there were any number of hiding places.

The bus took her out to the suburb in which her parents now lived. Their sheltered accommodation was inside a gated community, although, whether the gates were to keep out undesirables or to stop the residents wandering off, they were wide open and Jessie was able to just walk through. There was no kind of gatehouse, just a lamplit sign asking visitors to report to reception, which Jessie ignored. She could see her parents' front door and made her way towards it. Not having been there before, when she knocked on their door she felt like a stranger; she was not sure that she had not made a mistake. She looked again at the signs at the entrance and at the number on the door of this house that was her parents' but which was not her home. She got ready to apologise to whoever answered the door, to say sorry for having disturbed them. The door opened and there was her mother, saying, 'It's rather late.'

'I'm sorry,' said Jessie.

'Well, come inside,' said her mother. 'I've got tea ready. We've been waiting.'

Jessie came into the hallway and put down her travel bag.

'You're not staying here, are you?' said her mother. 'I haven't got a bed ready for you.'

'No,' said Jessie, 'Gail will come and fetch me.'

'There is a spare room,' said her mother, indicating one of the closed doors, 'but your dad uses it for his jigsaw puzzles.'

In the front room, their family photographs were displayed against unfamiliar wallpaper. Their old living-room curtains were hanging at the bungalow's bay window, though they did not quite fit. Her dad was waiting in his favourite armchair next to a fireplace, with his carriage clock ticking away on the mantelpiece, and the standard lamp with its faded shade standing like a sentry beside him.

'Hello, Dad,' said Jessie.

'It's about time,' he said.

Jessie sat down on the sofa, and the ancient cats appeared from nowhere to wind around her ankles. There was an exchange of Christmas gifts – Jessie received a set of stationery and a set of bath salts – and then her mother said, 'Are you hungry?' The five o'clock tea was laid out on a table in the corner.

'I'm starving,' said Jessie.

'You're not starving,' said her mother. 'You're just hungry.'

She took Jessie over to the table. The tea was like the food at a children's birthday party. The triangular, white-bread sandwiches had their crusts cut off – 'You still like jam, don't you?' asked her mother – and the little cakes were iced and sprinkled with hundreds and thousands. They filled their plates and sat back down.

'What time's Gail coming?' asked her mother.

Jessie, through a mouthful of tomato sandwich, said, 'Soon, I think.'

'I put the crusts on the bird table,' said her mother.

'Do you get many birds on it?' asked Jessie. They would not be out at this time, she thought; they would be safely up in the trees, away from the neighbourhood cats, away from her parents' own cats.

'None yet,' said her mother, 'but they'll come when they're hungry enough.'

'We've got a family roosting in the eaves,' said her dad.

'Your dad wants to stop them nesting there,' said her mother.

'They make such a mess,' said her dad.

'Well I like them,' said her mother.

'I might have something nesting in my eaves,' said Jessie. That might be all it was, that scratching sound: birds in her eaves. It was a common problem.

'Are you going to get rid of yours?' asked her dad.

'Leave them alone,' said her mother.

'I think it's birds, anyway,' said Jessie. 'My neighbour says if it isn't birds it's a ghost!'

Her mother looked at her. 'What time did you say Gail was coming?' she asked.

'Soon, I think,' said Jessie.

They all heard the sound of a car outside and turned their heads towards the window, but it wasn't Gail; the car went past.

'It's an old house, of course,' Jessie went on. 'You know it's the same house Lenore lived in, my great-great-grandmother?'

'No, it's not,' said her mother. 'That house is long gone.'

'No,' said Jessie, 'it's the same one you pointed out when I was little, when we were driving back from Loch Ness.'

'You must have been looking in the wrong direction,' said her mother. 'Your great-great-grandmother's house was knocked down a long time ago, in the late eighteen hundreds. They've built something else there now. You're on the other side of the road.'

'How old's the house you're in?' asked her dad. 'Is it old enough to have ghosts?'

Jessie did not know how old it was, and besides, she saw no reason why a modern house should not also have its ghosts; perhaps a modern house would come with the ghosts of whatever had stood there before, ghosts that might resent the new house and the living.

'That's enough,' said her mother. The sound of a car engine outside made her turn to the window again. 'Is that Gail?'

When she saw that it wasn't Gail, Jessie's mother stood and began to collect the tea things onto a tray, while Jessie, trying to help, got in the way and spilt the milk.

'Where's Will?' asked her dad.

'Didn't Gail tell you?' said Jessie.

'She said something to your mother. I can't say I understand,' he said, as if they had been playing the game in which something reasonably sensible was whispered from one person to another and then to another and somewhere along the line became unfathomable.

The third car was Gail's. Their mother, on the doorstep, said to her, 'Are you coming in?'

'Not today,' said Gail. 'We've got Michael and Linda with us, and I promised I wouldn't be gone very long.'

Michael was a cousin of theirs, once removed or twice removed. Jessie did not quite understand the meaning, but she had always found it an unsettling term: when she was a child, she had found the idea of him - the idea of him being *removed* - disturbing.

She had not seen him for years.

While Jessie got her things together, her mother carried

the tray of leftovers from the living room into the hallway. 'These can go on the bird table,' she said.

'You shouldn't be giving the birds white bread and cake,' said Gail. 'It's bad for them.'

But their mother, as if she had not heard, carried on towards the kitchen with her offerings.

Gail turned to Jessie and said, 'Are you ready then?'

'I'm ready,' said Jessie, reaching for her travel bag. 'Oh,' she said, 'I nearly forgot.' She unzipped the side pocket and took out the piece of sky. Her mother came back into the hallway, and Jessie, showing her, said, 'I found it.'

'Where on earth did you find that?' asked her mother.

'It was in my laundry basket,' said Jessie.

Her mother wanted to know how it had got in there, but Jessie could not say. 'Show your dad,' she said. Her dad was already coming closer, putting his glasses on, wanting to see what all the excitement was about.

'I found the missing piece,' said Jessie, holding it out so that her dad could see it.

He took the corner of blue sky carefully from Jessie and examined it like a jeweller assessing a diamond. For a terrible moment, she thought he might say that wasn't it, that it was not the piece he had been looking for. 'You've found it,' he said. 'Good girl.' He turned away, going down the hallway and into the spare room, closing the door behind him.

'He'll be able to finish it now,' said Jessie's mother. 'We'll be able to put it away in its box. He can start another one.'

'You've eaten, then?' asked Gail, as they drove away from the bungalow.

'Yes,' said Jessie. 'Mum made her five o'clock tea. I've had jam and tomato sandwiches.'

'Jam and tomato?' said Gail.

'Yes,' said Jessie.

Gail pulled a face. 'We ate with Michael and Linda,' she said. 'They came over for dinner. They're not staying over; there isn't anywhere for them to sleep.'

There was Eleanor's bedroom, but Jessie did not say this to Gail.

'Linda's got good news,' said Gail. 'She's pregnant. It's the very early stages, so she has to be careful. Normally, she wouldn't have told anyone yet, but she told us, and she said to tell you as well, so that you would know to be careful.'

Gail lived in the same suburban area in which they had grown up. She made a series of familiar turns, driving slowly down the empty streets. Beyond the deserted primary school, she pulled into her driveway. Jessie saw the Christmas tree in the front window, the twinkling of its many tiny lights.

'It seems like a long time since I was here,' said Jessie.

'It is a long time,' said Gail. 'You haven't been here since New Year. You haven't been back since the party.'

Jessie carried her travel bag to the door and Gail let them into the hallway. 'I'll go and see if Gary's all right with the washing up,' she said, heading towards the kitchen. 'You go into the living room – Michael and Linda are in there.'

'Shall I come and say hello to Gary first?' asked Jessie.

'I'll tell him you're here,' said Gail. 'You go through. I'll bring you a drink.'

Jessie went into the living room, where Michael and Linda were sitting on the sofa. When they saw Jessie, they stood to meet her. 'Don't get up,' said Jessie, but they were already up.

She hugged Michael, and then very carefully hugged Linda. 'Congratulations,' she said. Her hand had gone, very gently, to Linda's stomach, and Linda took a step backwards, covering her stomach with her own hand.

'Please don't,' said Linda.

'Sorry,' said Jessie.

Linda and Michael returned to their seats, and Jessie followed them, taking the free end of the sofa. The journey and the visit to her parents' house had tired her out, and perhaps she sat down too heavily, too close to Linda. Both Michael and Gail, who was coming into the room with a glass of wine, said, 'Be careful, Jessie.' Linda shifted an inch or two away, and Jessie recalled a *New Scientist* article that she had read, about how fetuses could learn to recognise the predators that they would need to avoid.

'Linda wants a girl,' said Gail. To Linda, she added, 'I really hope it will be.'

Jessie had barely started her wine when Michael and Linda decided they were ready to leave. 'I need my sleep now,' said Linda.

'Quite right,' said Gail. 'You need to look after this little girl.'

Gail was to drive them home as they were without a car and it was raining. At the door, Gary took out a pack of cigars. That was what he smoked: cigars rather than cigarettes, as if there were always new babies to celebrate, which of course there were. Gary handed a cigar to Michael, who took it, though he said it was a bit early for such things. 'I'll keep it,' he said, 'until the baby arrives.'

They left, and Gary went back into the kitchen. Jessie returned to the living room and her glass of wine.

Gail had been gone for about ten minutes when Jessie heard someone singing at the door: a child, she thought, carol singing, even though Christmas had passed. She wondered if the child didn't sound rather young to be out so late. She waited for Gary to go to the door, but she did not hear him. She could hear the child's voice coming through the glass and down the hallway:

*O bring us some figgy pudding*
*O bring us some figgy pudding*
*O bring us some figgy pudding*
*and bring it right here.*

She wondered if anyone had figgy pudding these days; she was not even entirely sure what it was. Well, of course, that was not really what the child wanted; it wanted sweets or money. Or no, she thought, that was Halloween. The child wanted money: this was like Halloween but without the sweets. She could hear the child chanting:

*We won't go until we've got some*
*We won't go until we've got some*
*We won't go until we've got some*
*so bring some out here.*

She did not want to go out there, but she could not hear Gary going, and the child needed money, then it could leave. Jessie got to her feet and went out to the hallway. 'Gary?' she said. She could see the kitchen – the sink, the running dishwasher, the clear surfaces – from where she was, but she could not see Gary. Nonetheless, she walked down the hallway to the kitchen doorway. 'Gary?' she said, though she could see that he was not there.

She turned back to the front door. She could see the child's face, blurred and distorted by the window and by the rain on the glass. She could not see an adult standing with it. Jessie's shoulder bag was hanging on a peg by the door. She would pay the child and then it would move on.

She took some coins from her purse, opened the door and saw – standing on the rain-wet doorstep – Paul, with a begging tin in his hand. Except that this boy was eight or nine years old, and, as he held his tin out towards her, a woman moved into the light and Jessie recognised Amy. Jessie had heard that Amy and Brendan were back together, married with a child, as if that summer had never happened, as if any wrongdoing on Jessie's part had been erased, or so she liked to think. Jessie dropped her coins into the tin, at the bottom of which rainwater had collected; it was like dropping change into a tiny wishing well. She wanted to give him more, but while she was reaching back into her shoulder bag, Amy was taking his hand and leading him away. Jessie watched them walk to the next house, where the boy took a deep breath and sang again.

Jessie was still in the hallway when Gail's car pulled into the driveway, and at the same time Gary came in from the garden, through the back door, smelling of his cigar smoke. He came into the hallway as Gail came in through the front door.

'I'm going up,' said Gary, looking past Jessie – looking *through* her, it felt like – at his wife.

'You're going to bed?' asked Gail.

'I'll read,' said Gary, who was already climbing the stairs.

Gail and Jessie stayed downstairs for a while longer, and

then Gail, collecting up the glasses and cups from the coffee table, said, 'Perhaps we should all turn in.'

She took Jessie up to the spare room and switched on the bedside lamp. 'Here's your towel,' said Gail, who always put one out for her, at the end of the bed, and Jessie thought of *The Hitchhiker's Guide to the Galaxy* and the towel that you would always want to have with you when travelling through space.

'Gary and I will be off to work early tomorrow,' said Gail, 'but you'll be all right, won't you? You can help yourself to breakfast and you know your way around.' She checked that Jessie had her travel bag and that she would need nothing more, and then, saying goodnight, she closed the door.

In the morning, after showering and dressing and dealing with her hair, Jessie went down to the kitchen and looked for fruit, but she could only find tins, and no tin opener. She ate the bread that Gail had left out for her, put a bottle of water into her shoulder bag, and left the house. She pulled the door firmly to behind her, but still when she reached the end of the driveway she went back to check it.

She took a bus into the city centre and walked the route she had walked many times before, past all the places that had once displayed their flyers – *Missing . . .* – which had over time become rain-damaged and had now disappeared altogether.

At the museum, she visited the exhibits, the cafe and the gift shop and the toilets. Inside her orange cubicle, she said quietly, 'Stay here. Talk to me so I know you're there.'

Over dinner, she told Gail where she had been, and Gary said, 'What *for*? What do you go there *for*? She isn't there, you won't find her there.'

The following day, Gail stayed at home with Jessie, although Gary went to work again, leaving the house early. Gail and Jessie went for a walk by the river. Gail asked after Will, and Jessie mentioned the postcards.

'He's still in touch, then?' said Gail.

'Just about,' said Jessie.

At lunchtime, they drank wine, and Jessie told Gail that her period was more than a week late.

'It was the same with me,' said Gail.

'You mean with Eleanor?' asked Jessie.

'What?' said Gail. 'I mean the menopause. A few years ago, I was expecting my period to come as normal, and at first I just thought it was late, and then it never came, and that was that.'

Jessie returned to Gail's house with a headache. Looking in the bathroom cabinet for painkillers, she found an unused pregnancy testing kit. She opened the box.

Throughout the soup, Jessie prepared to tell her sister. She was not sure how she would react, but she thought of Linda; she thought of Gail being happy and protective, and of Gary's celebratory cigar. It was hard to believe that, after all this time, she could once again be in the club.

In between the soup and the beef bourguignon, Jessie said, 'I took a pregnancy test and it was positive. Faint but positive.'

Gail took a moment to swallow her mouthful of beef. 'That's very unlikely,' she said.

'It's unexpected,' agreed Jessie.

Gary said to Gail, 'Is Will back?'

Gail shook her head and Jessie said, 'I've been seeing someone new. His name's Robert.'

'You've not mentioned him before,' said Gail, as if there were something suspicious about it, as if he might be imaginary. 'You can't be pregnant. It's impossible. You're nearly fifty.'

'It's not impossible,' said Jessie. 'It happens.'

'You can't be,' insisted Gail. 'You shouldn't be.'

Gary said nothing. He continued to eat, as if she had not spoken. When he had finished eating, he took his plate into the kitchen.

There was to be another New Year's Eve party to which Jessie had been invited and which she had expected to attend, but she decided not to stay. 'I wouldn't be drinking anyway,' she said.

'You're not pregnant,' said Gail, 'get that idea out of your head,' as if thinking it or not thinking it could make a baby come or go.

Jessie texted Robert from the train. *I'm on my way home*, she wrote. He had not replied when she texted again to say, *I'm late*. This was, she realised – as she pressed the little envelope icon, sending the message through the ether – ambiguous in the circumstances, and she composed a third text saying, *I think I'm pregnant*. She added a smiley face, and then was unsure; she deleted the smiley face and sent the message.

She did not hear back from Robert.

By the time she got off the bus in Hawick, it had been dark for hours, but Morrisons was still open and she went in to buy fruit and other perishables. She filled her basket and then, on the way home, wondered if she would be able to get through it all before it spoiled.

There was post on her doormat. There was a postcard from Bruges, from Will. The two of them were once in Bruges together. There had been a plague of insects, flying ants, which settled on their arms, their legs, their clothes; they got into Jessie's hair and in between the pages of the book that she had been trying to read. This postcard did not say that he was coming, that he was on his way; it said he liked it in Bruges.

The dog and the cat were pleased to see her. She asked them, 'Has Robert been looking after you?' She looked to see if he had left her a note, but there was nothing.

She spent Hogmanay in The Bourtree. She drank orange juice and came home early, without having seen Robert. Of course, the original plan had been for her to spend the night at her sister's house, to be at her sister's party, and Robert had obviously made his own plans that involved being elsewhere. She had invited Robert to the party but he had refused to be drawn into her family circle; his own family was quite enough, he said. 'You go on your own,' he told her. 'You need me here to look after the animals anyway.' She imagined him now being somewhere remote, somewhere deep in the countryside or night diving, somewhere he could not get a signal.

Lying in bed, she counted the weeks, through the winter – when everything seemed dead but was really only resting – and into the coming spring. The fetus should be viable by the beginning of May, the month of Beltane, a time of year when, traditionally, livestock were driven out to pasture, protected from harm by fire rituals that appeased the spirits that lived underground or across the sea or in an invisible world existing alongside the human world.

The old year slipped away and the new year came in while Jessie was sleeping.

In the morning, she sent a text message to everyone in her phone's contact list. The message said, *Happy New Year!!* and after it she added kisses, crosses. It would go to Gail. If it reached Paul, he would not reply. It would not go to Will, for whom she had no number. It would go to Robert, who might be somewhere without a signal but who would receive it eventually. It was only after she had pressed send that she realised that it would also go to Alasdair.

On the second of January, Jessie went to Morrisons, needing tinned and frozen food that would make her arms ache on the way home. She was in the freezer aisle, deliberating over the vegetables – thinking of her peas in Robert's freezer, thinking, though, that they would be all right in there for months – when an arm reaching into the chest and taking out a bag of something frozen made her glance up. There was Robert, no more than a metre away. She was on the verge of saying his name, but she was suddenly so sure that he had seen her and was choosing not to look her way that his name got stuck in her throat; it would not come out. He was turning away now: she saw the frozen roast potatoes in his basket, and watched as he walked to the end of the aisle and went out of sight. She could not believe that he had not seen her. She had been blanked. She thought of her unanswered text messages – there were new ways to be blanked nowadays; they called it ghosting. She had to hold on to the edge of the vegetable freezer.

Perhaps her reading of the situation was wrong though. Perhaps he had not seen her after all. Perhaps he had only been thinking about his vegetables, his roast potatoes, about getting them home and into his freezer. Perhaps *she* was the one who had seen *him* and failed to speak. She *had* seen him and failed to speak.

Letting go of the freezer, she headed for the front of the shop, where she scanned the checkouts but could not see him. From the exit, she spotted him striding across the car park with his single bag of shopping, and hurried to catch him up.

'Robert?' she said.

He kept walking, looking dead ahead.

'Thank you for looking after the animals,' she said. She tried to walk alongside him even though the speed was uncomfortable for her. 'I hope they behaved themselves for you. I hope the *house* behaved itself too.'

'Just stop it, Jessie,' he said.

'What?' she said.

'Your house is just a house,' said Robert. 'There is no ghost.' He did not slow his pace or turn to face her. 'You have an old house that needs some attention. The door in your spare room needs rehanging. Your windows need new putty – or get some double glazing. And I already told you, I don't want a kid.'

Jessie came to a stop. While Robert marched on, Jessie felt a hand on her shoulder, and she turned to see a man in uniform, and in her own hand was a basket of shopping for which she had not paid.

They used to make single women give up their babies; they used to take the babies away, and that was not so long ago. Or at least they did when the women were young; Jessie was no longer young.

She went online and did a search: 'abortion clinic Hawick'. She clicked on a link. *We are sorry*, said the computer. *There are no abortion clinics in the Scottish Borders.* She tried again. *We are sorry*, said the computer. *There are no abortion clinics in Scotland.* She would try again. *We are sorry*, the computer would say. *There are no abortion clinics.* But a different search discovered an abundance: a clinic in Glasgow, another in Newcastle-upon-Tyne. She had a choice. Each one was some hours away. She would have to catch the bus and then the train. Or not. She did not know who would look after the animals.

She had only ever known one person to go to an abortion clinic, and that person had not, in the end, gone through with it: she had got as far as the waiting room – and that, thought Jessie, would be the worst bit, waiting for it to happen – and then she had turned around and gone home again. Jessie could imagine doing just that. Months later, this same girl, walking through town, had bumped into the father, who spoke to her quite normally whilst never once acknowledging the baby lying in the pram between them.

Having abandoned her New Year shop and having, in the intervening days, felt unable to go back to Morrisons, Jessie had run out of fruit.

She had toast for breakfast, and dithered over whether to have jam or the new marmalade, which she had found – which she must mistakenly have placed – in the freezer. Physicists, so she had read, were coming to the conclusion that this universe was only one of an infinite number, and that all possible versions of her and her life existed somewhere. In this universe she might have jam and in another she would have marmalade, and in yet another she would have eggs, which she had not even got.

She cleared the junk out of the spare room. Vacuuming under the bed, getting right into the corner, she found her missing pieces of jewellery, which must have worked their way loose and fallen to the floor on nights when, unable to sleep, she had visited this cold little room in search of Eleanor. She put the locket back around her neck, the watch back around her wrist, the hooks of the turquoise earrings through the holes in her ears. She also found her wedding ring, but she was not sure what to do with that.

She washed the dusty blanket and hung it on the line to dry before taking the dog out. On her way through town, she paused to knock on Robert's door, though he was never there. She walked on, as far as the surgery. She kept a wary eye on the overcast sky, thinking of her blanket on the line, but she could see that the sun was trying to come out, and indeed, in the time that she was in the ear clinic, the clouds parted. As she walked the dog home, with a new clarity in her ear, her sense of being muffled and separate began to retreat. She had a feeling of reconnection, as if she had been underwater and was finally surfacing.

The brightening morning was so springlike that she wondered if, on returning home, she might see buds on her plants. She could sit at the window, looking into the garden. She had a new life of Lawrence to begin. She would turn a page and find him newborn; he would once again be young and spirited.

*I* MEANT TO *be home long before now. I imagined return-*
*ing in the late autumn fog, out of which I would emerge as*
*Jessie stood in the doorway, waiting for me; or leaving footprints*
*in a Christmas frost as I crossed the yard. But I have been gone*
*from one year to the next and when I finally arrive – with*
*a John Denver song in my head, 'Take Me Home, Country*
*Roads' – Jessie is not standing in the doorway. The door is*
*closed; it is locked.*

*I take out my key and insert it into the lock. When I turn*
*it, a part of me expects to find that it will not move, to find that*
*the locks have been changed. But the key turns and the door*
*opens, allowing me in.*

*I enter and call out, 'Jessie?' but there is no answer. I walk*
*further into the house and call again, but there is no response.*
*The house is cold. The first thing I will do is see to the heating.*

*The dog's food bowl is empty. I call, but the dog does not*
*come either.*

*The postcards I sent are on the kitchen windowsill, although*
*the most recent one at least is missing and maybe never arrived.*
*I take a look at the kitchen calendar, trying to think what day it*
*is; I've lost track. I fix on a square in the middle of the month,*
*which I think could be today, either today or tomorrow. There's*
*a note in Jessie's handwriting, in pencil: a departure time. All*
*the squares beyond it are blank.*

*The house is quiet, apart from the sound of it trying to settle.*

# ACKNOWLEDGEMENTS

A S EVER, I'M indebted to my editor Nick Royle and my husband Dan for their careful readings of this novel, for astute feedback and for helping to iron out my lumps and bumps. I am also grateful to Dan for his constant love and support, and for his patient description of a nighttime visit to a creepy abandoned convalescent home with his camera. Thanks to Jen and Chris Hamilton-Emery at Salt, who continue to be brilliantly supportive and enabling. Thanks to my son, Arthur, for never being short of ideas and hugs. Thanks to Sarah, Chris and Emily, for hosting us and exploring with us in the Scottish Borders. And thanks to the other Nick Royle, at the University of Sussex, for pointing me towards Mark Twain's essay 'Mental Telegraphy'.

I have drawn on two D. H. Lawrence biographies: *Flame into Being: The Life and Work of D. H. Lawrence* by Anthony Burgess, and *D. H. Lawrence: The Life of an Outsider* by John Worthen. My line 'the wind muttered at the window and the trees shook off the last of their leaves' is a nod to D. H. Lawrence's poem 'At the Window'. I have quoted from Robert Browning's version of *The Pied Piper of Hamelin*. I have described the work of the German children's author Jutta Bauer, specifically *Schreimutter* and *Opa's Engel*. The short story that Jessie refers to in Intercourse is

'Observations About Eggs From the Man Sitting Next to Me on a Flight From Chicago, Illinois to Cedar Rapids, Iowa' by Carmen Maria Machado in *Year's Best Weird Fiction*, Vol. 2, eds. Kathe Koja and Michael Kelly, Undertow Publications.

# NEW FICTION FROM SALT

RON BUTLIN
*Billionaires' Banquet* (978-1-78463-100-0)

NEIL CAMPBELL
*Sky Hooks* (978-1-78463-037-9)

SUE GEE
*Trio* (978-1-78463-061-4)

CHRISTINA JAMES
*Rooted in Dishonour* (978-1-78463-089-8)

V.H. LESLIE
*Bodies of Water* (978-1-78463-071-3)

WYL MENMUIR
*The Many* (978-1-78463-048-5)

ANNA STOTHARD
*The Museum of Cathy* (978-1-78463-082-9)

ALSO AVAILABLE FROM SALT

ELIZABETH BAINES
*Too Many Magpies* (978-1-84471-721-7)
*The Birth Machine* (978-1-907773-02-0)

LESLEY GLAISTER
*Little Egypt* (978-1-907773-72-3)

ALISON MOORE
*The Lighthouse* (978-1-907773-17-4)
*The Pre-War House and Other Stories* (978-1-907773-50-1)
*He Wants* (978-1-907773-81-5)
*Death and the Seaside* (978-1-78463-069-0)

ALICE THOMPSON
*Justine* (978-1-78463-031-7)
*The Falconer* (978-1-78463-009-6)
*The Existential Detective* (978-1-78463-011-9)
*Burnt Island* (978-1-907773-48-8)
*The Book Collector* (978-1-78463-043-0)

RECENT FICTION FROM SALT

KERRY HADLEY-PRYCE
*The Black Country* (978-1-78463-034-8)

CHRISTINA JAMES
*The Crossing* (978-1-78463-041-6)

IAN PARKINSON
*The Beginning of the End* (978-1-78463-026-3)

CHRISTOPHER PRENDERGAST
*Septembers* (978-1-907773-78-5)

JONATHAN TAYLOR
*Melissa* (978-1-78463-035-5)

GUY WARE
*The Fat of Fed Beasts* (978-1-78463-024-9)

NEW BOOKS FROM SALT

XAN BROOKS
*The Clocks in This House All Tell Different Times*
(978-1-78463-093-5)

MICKEY J C ORRIGAN
*Project XX* (978-1-78463-097-3)

MARIE GAMESON
*The Giddy Career of Mr Gadd (deceased)*
(978-1-78463-118-5)

LESLEY GLAISTER
*The Squeeze* (978-1-78463-116-1)

NAOMI HAMILL
*How To Be a Kosovan Bride* (978-1-78463-095-9)

CHRISTINA JAMES
*Fair of Face* (978-1-78463-108-6)

This book has been typeset by
SALT PUBLISHING LIMITED
using Neacademia, a font designed by Sergei Egorov
for the Rosetta Type Foundry in the Czech Republic.
It is manufactured using Creamy 70gsm, a Forest
Stewardship Council™ certified paper from Stora Enso's
Anjala Mill in Finland. It was printed and bound by
Clays Limited in Bungay, Suffolk, Great Britain.

CROMER
GREAT BRITAIN
MMXVIII